KNIFE AT A GUNFIGHT

Fargo aimed his Colt and looked at Stover, everything in his face smiling except those unblinking lake-blue eyes. "Don't overrate yourself, Dill," he warned. Stover paled beneath his beard scruff.

Turkey Neck chose that moment to make his play, expecting Stover to back him. Even as he slapped for his hog-leg pistol, Fargo flipped his Colt into his left hand and raised his right leg, snatching the Arkansas Toothpick from his boot.

All this happened in an eye blink. Turkey Neck's big pistol cleared leather even as Fargo's right arm hurled the blade at him in a streaking blur. The Toothpick punched deep into the man's chest before he could fire a shot. He twitched a few times, coughed up a gout of blood, then slid from the saddle like a sack of grain.

THE TRAILSMAN

#285

SALT LAKE SLAUGHTER

by

Jon Sharpe

A SIGNET BOOK

SIGNET
Published by New American Library, a division of
Penguin Group (USA) Inc., 375 Hudson Street,
New York, New York 10014, USA
Penguin Group (Canada), 10 Alcorn Avenue, Toronto,
Ontario M4V 3B2, Canada (a division of Pearson Penguin Canada Inc.)
Penguin Books Ltd., 80 Strand, London WC2R 0RL, England
Penguin Ireland, 25 St. Stephen's Green, Dublin 2,
Ireland (a division of Penguin Books Ltd.)
Penguin Group (Australia), 250 Camberwell Road, Camberwell, Victoria 3124,
Australia (a division of Pearson Australia Group Pty. Ltd.)
Penguin Books India Pvt. Ltd., 11 Community Centre, Panchsheel Park,
New Delhi - 110 017, India
Penguin Group (NZ), cnr Airborne and Rosedale Roads, Albany,
Auckland 1310, New Zealand (a division of Pearson New Zealand Ltd.)
Penguin Books (South Africa) (Pty.) Ltd., 24 Sturdee Avenue,
Rosebank, Johannesburg 2196, South Africa

Penguin Books Ltd., Registered Offices:
80 Strand, London WC2R 0RL, England

First published by Signet, an imprint of New American Library,
a division of Penguin Group (USA) Inc.

First Printing, July 2005
10 9 8 7 6 5 4 3 2 1

The first chapter of this book previously appeared in *Dakota Prairie Pirates,* the
two hundred eighty-fourth volume in this series.

PUBLISHER'S NOTE
This is a work of fiction. Names, characters, places, and incidents either are the
product of the author's imagination or are used fictitiously, and any resemblance
to actual persons, living or dead, business establishments, events, or locales is
entirely coincidental.

The Trailsman

Beginnings . . . they bend the tree and they mark the man. Skye Fargo was born when he was eighteen. Terror was his midwife, vengeance his first cry. Killing spawned Skye Fargo, ruthless, cold-blooded murder. Out of the acrid smoke of gunpowder still hanging in the air, he rose, cried out a promise never forgotten.

The Trailsman they began to call him all across the West: searcher, scout, hunter, the man who could see where others only looked, his skills for hire but not his soul, the man who lived each day to the fullest, yet trailed each tomorrow. Skye Fargo, the Trailsman, the seeker who could take the wildness of a land and the wanting of a woman and make them his own.

Utah Territory, 1859—where the profit-and-loss ledgers are written in blood, and Fargo is keeping accounts.

1

"We won't die," the pretty brunette announced in a voice rubbed raw by thirst and grit. "A stranger is coming. A tall man who has no more fear in him than a rifle."

"Yes," snapped John Beckmann, her brother-in-law, "and every Jack shall have his Jill, too. *No one* is going to ride in and save us, Dora. This is real life, not some penny dreadful."

They were crossing a vast desert plain between scarred ranges of sterile mountains. The wind-driven grit felt like buckshot, and a blazing yellow sun was stuck high in the sky as if pegged there. Alkali dust hung curtain thick in the air, the searing sunlight turning it into a blinding white haze.

"The gateway to California," Beckmann said bitterly even as he staggered and almost fell. He was a thin, intelligent looking, sickly man dressed in sober black. "This is all my fault. In all the blowing dust, I fear I missed the place where the California Trail veers west from the Bear River. Like a fool, I swore by the Hastings guidebook as if it were Scripture, I—"

"John, there's no point in repeating all that," gently admonished his wife, Estelline, who was at least seven months along with child.

But Beckmann didn't seem to hear her. "No way to fight shy of the southern route through the Utah deserts, that infernal book insists, if we wish to avoid being caught by snow in the Sierra. I should have asked others. Now look— I've killed my own family!"

One of the children, four-year-old Lloyd, began crying, and wearily John picked up the exhausted boy. Three more small children trudged through the salt desert waste.

"We're all still very much alive, John," Estelline managed bravely. "But our mouths feel stuffed with cotton."

"No water since yesterday, that's why. Not to mention your empty bellies, rock-torn feet, and going half blind from the cursed glare," John replied.

It broke his heart to see Estelline, Dora, and the little ones trudging through this hellish landscape afoot. What sorry grass he'd found was so salt-encrusted the stock couldn't eat it. Deliberately poisoned water holes hastened the deaths of their yoke oxen and butcher beef.

"I was fully prepared to see my school in Los Angeles fail," he admitted. "The place is a lick-skittle settlement. But I always believed we'd at least make it out there—"

"We'll make it because help is coming," Dora insisted again. She held up a round crystal glass mounted in a glazed porcelain base. "My peeping stone never lies."

"Miracles, I believe in," Beckmann muttered. "But not devil-inspired sorcery."

"Doesn't matter if you believe," she replied. "Miracle or magic, a tall stranger *is* coming. And water with him."

Dora was pretty and petite like her older sister Estelline. She had lively green eyes and mother-of-pearl skin. Despite their desperate situation, her jet-black hair hung in two long braids tied with white ribbons in front of each shoulder. Her flowered muslin dress had been pretty before the salt dust coated it.

Beckmann cast a baleful glance around, his eyes trembling and watering—the salt desert hardpan produced a glare that could drive animals and humans mad. Back east, Salt Lake was being called "the Half Way House" between the Missouri River and the Pacific Ocean. All he'd found, so far, was a harsh, unforgiving land of tarantulas, centipedes, and scorpions. In this desolate salt-desert waste, no joyous birds celebrated sunup. It was an arid land of *borrasca*, barren rock.

A land of the dead. And soon—perhaps even within hours now—his own family's bones would be bleaching among the rest.

A worried Skye Fargo sleeved sweat out of his eyes, wondering if he and the Ovaro were at the end of their last trail.

2

The country he'd been traversing, the Great Basin of the Utah Territory, was so wide open he could almost see tomorrow. It was mostly barren desert plains crosshatched by equally barren mountains. Jagged volcanic rock loomed black against the sky.

Fargo knew this area as the western limit of the U.S. Army's vast Department of the Platte. Ten years ago, as a contract scout, he had led a detail of military surveyors and mapmakers through the Wasatch Range. Mountain Utes laid siege to them, and only a few well-aimed "smudge pots" (fire bombs made for tossing) frightened them off.

Fargo, whom some called the Trailsman, had explored this region before and knew how to survive in it. Still, it didn't help when some cowardly would-be assassin had deliberately poisoned his water supply a week ago at a Humboldt River outpost west of here. And Fargo, though lacking proof, had a good idea who had done it: Dill Stover, a barracks-room bully who pretended to be a soldier only to advance his criminal schemes.

Buckskins and beard powdered white from the alkali soil, Fargo led his played-out pinto stallion by the bridle reins. Fargo had lost his bearings in the last dust storm, but hoped like hell he was on the right path to reach the huge snow-melt reservoir at Mormon Station.

"That's the gait, old campaigner," Fargo remarked when the stallion lifted his nose into the furnace-hot wind. "We've got red sons all around us."

The Ovaro was trained to alert at the odor of bear grease, which many Indians smeared into their hair. Fargo knew he would require every possible warning because, unexpectedly, this entire region was crawling with warpath Indians.

This was terrain so hostile that even the mission padres gave it wide berth. Normally the Great Basin was empty except for a few nomadic braves, mostly Utes and a few Paiutes or Shoshonis. Lately, though, somebody had been selling guns, ammo, and liquor to the Utes. Now they were spreading terror through simultaneous raids on stage stations, mail riders, and freighters.

The Ovaro's ears pricked forward and Fargo drew his Colt, palming the wheel to check the loads. He'd rather face trouble on a tired horse than afoot, so Fargo stepped up into leather and loosened his brass-frame Henry in its boot.

"Keep up the strut," he urged the Ovaro, shortening the reins in case of trouble.

The pinto, like his master, was seriously dehydrated. Yet he brought his head up without fighting the bit, ready for the next scrape.

The wind rose to a shrieking howl, blasting Fargo's face with hard-driven grit and greatly reducing visibility. The brutal afternoon sun coaxed out a thick layer of sweat that mixed with the dust coating his skin, forming an irritating paste.

The Ovaro alerted again. Fargo, spotting dim shapes ahead in the swirling confusion, reached for his Henry, then checked the motion, his bearded jaw dropping open in astonishment.

"Dill goddamn Stover," he said aloud, the words surprised out of him.

The wind abated, and a strange sight revealed itself. Stover, in civilian clothes, sat his handsome roan gelding to one side of a buckboard heaped high with goods, including water casks. Stover bristled with arms: a shotgun, several revolvers, crossed bandoleers of bullets. A similarly armed guard covered the other side of the conveyance.

A driver wearing a broadcloth suit, and a hat with a veil to protect his eyes from grit and glare, was dickering with a skinny man who looked dead on his feet—bare, bleeding feet, at that.

"Fifteen dollars for a *glass* of water?" the man exclaimed. "Sir, that's usury!"

"No, pilgrim, it's the going price for water in the desert," the driver replied.

Fargo gaped at the four children. The youngest was on the verge of passing out, as was the exhausted-looking woman who was obviously expecting a child. And that compact little brunette beside her was staring at Fargo as if he were the messiah arrived.

"Sir!" the man protested again. "We have no cash. We were robbed by a road gang east of here. At least give us water for the children."

"It's no skin off my ass what happens to those little shirttail brats. It's nothing personal, mister, just business disci-

4

pline. If I give charity to one family, they all demand it. I'll take trade if you're cash-strapped."

"We lost our team, wagon, everything, south of here."

Fargo recalled a ruggedly built prairie wagon, and the dead team nearby, he'd spotted earlier. Just then Dill Stover, who'd been idly picking his teeth with a twig, shifted his trouble-seeking eyes in Fargo's direction. For a moment, before he reacted, he paled as if seeing a ghost. *Figured me for dead by now,* Fargo told himself.

He started to raise the scattergun, but instantly Fargo's right fist was curled around deadly steel. He thumb-cocked the hammer.

"Raise that smoke pole one more inch, Dill," Fargo promised him, "and you'll be kissing Satan's ass in hell. Goes for you, too, mister."

This last was directed at the second guard, a turkey-necked man with shifty eyes. He let his half-removed repeating rifle fall back into its saddle sheath.

"Is this a holdup?" demanded the driver. He seemed more amused than annoyed.

" 'Pears to me you're the one doing the robbing," Fargo replied, riding slowly back to glance in the buckboard. It was filled with footgear, clothing, and all sorts of food, even airtight tins of oysters and caviar.

"No law against a man setting his own prices based on demand," the driver replied. He pushed the veil aside and watched Fargo with the steady, unblinking eyes of a rattler.

"Especially," Fargo added, "with somebody poisoning all the water holes around here, huh? Creates a helluva demand."

His eyes shifted to Stover, who sat in a silver-trimmed vaquero saddle he hadn't owned a week ago. "Just like somebody poisoned my water before I left the outpost at Mary's Station."

Stover's broad, blunt face twisted with insolence. "There was others there besides me. If I decide to kill a man, Fargo, I brace him toe to toe," his bullhorn voice rasped.

Fargo doubted that. Stover was shiftier than a creased buck. His tone right now was that of a man with an ax to grind, and clearly he meant to grind it until the wheel squeaked. Fargo had recently been forced to spend two months with the unlikable man, on a scouting expedition

5

to sight through a federal resupply road for the U.S. Army's Far West outposts.

A rainy-day poker game at Mary's Station on the Humboldt had evolved into a dollar-ante slugfest between soldiers and scouts, and Fargo found himself riding a streak. Private Stover accused him of peeking at the deadwood. In the ensuing scuffle Fargo had severely pistol-whipped Stover instead of killing him—a serious mistake.

That beating, Fargo realized, was cankering at Stover. And the shotgun barrel was slowly coming up.

"You deserted, huh?" Fargo asked.

Stover looked smug. "Three-month enlistment, know-it-all."

Fargo believed that much. The army had to offer such foolish contracts now that goldfields dotted the West and drew off manpower.

"Well, next time you poison my gutbag of water with strychnine," Fargo advised him, "don't leave a little of the powder as a clue."

Stover had been making a cigarette. He struck a match and leaned into the flame, eyes mocking Fargo.

"Folks talk you up pretty high, Fargo," he said. "But you best watch that mouth of yours, hear? A man can turn his tongue into a shovel and dig his own grave with it."

"The ass waggeth his ears." Fargo glanced at the driver. "How 'bout it, boss man? Some water all around, starting with the tads?"

"No one asked you to put your oar in my boat, mister. If these pilgrims pay up, they're welcome to drink."

The driver glanced at the brunette, who still looked quite tempting despite the wear and tear of this desert hell. "I'm even willing to be flexible on the payment method," he added.

"Mighty Christian of you." Fargo watched Turkey Neck from the corner of one eye. The heavily armed man had a larval face with the furtive, hunted look of an owlhoot. And he was gradually turning his horse so that he and Stover could burn Fargo in a crossfire play. Never mind, thought Fargo, how many women and kids they also mow down . . .

"You heading to Salt Lake for the big race, Fargo?" Stover suddenly jeered. "The big race the Mormons're put-tin' on? Me, I'd love to ride against you, cut you and that stallion down to size."

Who *hadn't* heard of the so-called Salt Lake Run, a grueling 120-mile horse race across brutal salt and volcanic-rock desert. No remounts allowed and no water except a tank at the halfway point and whatever the rider dared to carry. Besides a generous cash prize, the winner would be offered a lucrative contract to carry mail between Salt Lake City and the Mormon settlement of San Bernardino, California.

But Stover's question, Fargo realized, was only a diversion. A fox play was coming.

He looked at Stover, everything in Fargo's face smiling except those unblinking, lake-blue eyes. "Don't overrate yourself, Dill," he warned in a quiet, almost pleasant tone. The former soldier paled beneath his beard scruff.

Turkey Neck chose that moment to make his play, expecting Stover to back his hand. Even as he slapped for a hog-leg pistol in an underarm holster, Fargo flipped his Colt into his left hand and raised his right leg, snatching the Arkansas Toothpick from his boot.

All this happened in an eyeblink. Turkey Neck's big pistol cleared leather even as Fargo's right arm hurled the blade at him in a streaking blur. The Arkansas Toothpick punched deep into the man's chest before he could fire a shot. He twitched a few times, coughed up a gout of blood, then slid from the saddle like a sack of grain.

Fargo's Colt remained aimed at Stover, who sat stone still. But the Trailsman had forgotten about the driver of the buckboard—until he heard the loud, metallic click of a rifle being cocked.

2

"Good work, boss!" Dill Stover exclaimed, raising the twin muzzles of his scattergun toward Fargo. "Let's open the ball!"

Fargo ignored the odds and kept Stover covered, eyes boring into him like augers.

"I'm down to the sear pin with no trigger slack left, Dill," Fargo warned him. "Doesn't matter which one of you shoots me, the slightest twitch on this trigger and you're in the bullet's path."

"That's cow plop," Stover scoffed.

It sure's hell is, Fargo thought. But at the moment he had nothing better than bluff. And with bluff alone Fargo had cleaned out Stover in five-card stud.

"All right," Fargo invited, smiling with his lips only. "Tweak those triggers and find out."

"Think I won't, big man?"

Stover's weather-rawed face twisted with malevolent intent. But the granite-jawed, buckskin-clad man before him was the most unnerving bastard Stover had ever clashed with.

"Plug him, boss!" Stover shouted to the man in the buckboard, hoping to make Fargo flinch.

But Fargo remained steady as a stone church. And the well-dressed driver only laughed.

"Why *kill* him?" he demanded. "He stopped Pete and got the drop on you, didn't he? My supposed 'guards.' I only covered him to save your worthless hide, Dill. I require at least one guard to get back to Mormon Station."

The driver lowered his hammer and put the repeating rifle back under the seat.

Stover, on his own now, was suddenly so angry the bones stood out in his face. "But this bastard just cut down Pete!"

"Yes, and Pete Helzer was a worthless horse thief and debt-skipper who gave Mr. Fargo no warning. The Code, Dill, requires that a man make clear his intention to kill. But I doubt you know that."

"But Fargo already had his shooter out, and Pete—"

His employer waved him silent. "The matter is over. If it sticks in your craw, collect your wages right now."

He was still watching Fargo from amused eyes. "Why build a pimple into a peak, I say. Mr. Fargo, you're all grit and a yard wide. You looking for a job?"

"Well, kiss my lily-white ass!" Stover erupted. He was in a stew now, perhaps recalling his beating, at Fargo's hands, out west at Mary's Station. "You hire this peckerwood, Mr. Childress, you'll still be short a guard, on account I *will* quit!"

"With him on the payroll, Dill, I won't need two guards."

"Thanks for the offer," Fargo replied, "but I'm not the wage-hustling type. What say we dicker instead, Mr. Childress, on these inflated prices of yours? These folks need water, and in a puffin' hurry. I'm a mite dry myself."

"Inflated? A matter of perspective. Now, Mr. Fargo, surely you know how the extreme costs and risks of freighting goods makes them very costly throughout the Utah Territory."

This was true enough. Even the Mormons in Salt Lake City sold their excellent eggs and dairy products at astounding rates to emigrants on the California Trail.

"This area is the crossroads of a gold-strike region," Childress added. "The Comstock Lode to the west of us, Pikes Peak, Cherry Creek, and Cache la Poudre to the east—do you realize that sugar, tobacco, and coffee are literally worth their weight in gold in these places? Hell, some men pan color all day long just for their eats."

Fargo nodded. "I got nothing against reasonable profiteering," he replied. "But these ain't miners with plenty of gold, they're seven pilgrims who've lost everything, four of them kids."

Childress surrendered with a laugh. "Your eloquence, Mr. Fargo, shames me into doing my Christian duty. Belly up to the bar, folks! Drinks're on me."

Stover cursed as the Beckmann party rushed the buckboard, herding the kids before them. Thanks to Fargo's use of the Arkansas Toothpick, the children weren't even aware that the man curled up in the sand wasn't just sleeping.

When his turn came, Fargo first watered the Ovaro from his hat. Then he drank his fill and filled two canteens. Still flush with his recent poker winnings, he talked Childress into a generous discount on some loaves of saleratus bread, a slab of bacon, a few cans of peaches and tomatoes. Even with a discount, however, these meager rations cost forty dollars.

Stover eyed Fargo's roll of military script with anger and envy—much of it had once been his. "I've noticed, Fargo, you tend to win at cards most often when you deal."

"Your insults are all free shots now," Fargo told him mildly. "Our showdown was guaranteed when you poisoned my water. Won't be too long before one of us bucks out in smoke."

The mild tone could not disguise the lethal message. As Childress and his guard began to ride out, Stover slued around in his fancy vaquero saddle.

"Harken and heed, Fargo! If you hadn't snuck up on me from behind at Mary's Station, I'da whipped the snot outta you! It's past that now. Next time I'll kill you!"

Childress removed his broad-brimmed hat and saluted them. "Folks, I grant all of you clear title to hell!" he shouted, laughing hard and using his hat to indicate the burning wasteland surrounding them.

Fargo watched the buckboard shimmy away through the glaring white sand, his gaze thoughtful. Stover was the typical shifty-eyed hardtail found at every frontier outpost. But Childress . . . that was evil Fargo glimpsed in his pale-agate eyes, all right.

"We owe you a huge debt of gratitude, sir," said a voice at his elbow. "John Beckmann is the name."

Fargo gave the pale, sickly man a grip. "Skye Fargo. Mr. Beckmann, what in hell are you folks doing wandering all over Robin Hood's barn all alone? You're nowhere near a wagon road."

"We left too late in the season to join a larger party. According to my map, we should be following the California Trail as it skirts the north shore of Great Salt Lake."

"Well, now you're in a sweet little orchid garden called the Great Salt *Desert*," Fargo corrected him. "West of the lake and well south of the trail."

Fargo understood the situation when he realized the dog-eared volume Beckmann still carried was *The Emigrants' Guide to Oregon and California* by Lansford Hastings. Bad information had killed more greenhorns than Indians had.

"The Donner Party took the advice in that book, too," Fargo observed. "I recommend you use it for kindling. Along with its jackleg map of Salt Lake."

Fargo opened the book to the big map inside the cover. He pointed to the huge river flowing from Salt Lake to the Pacific. "You'll find no river. Salt Lake is landlocked."

Beckmann's face fell. "I finally realized this book is hogwash. But no fresh water nearby?"

"Utah Lake is fresh water, but it's well southeast of here near the Wasatch Range. And right now it's no safe haven for whiteskins—several tribes are on the scrap."

"Tribes?" Estelline repeated, alarm tightening her wan, weary face. "We were told back home in Iowa the Indians out here were mostly pacified."

"Oh? Well, at any moment we could be up to our armpits in 'pacified' redskins. Salt Lake City is safe, but Logan, Brigham, Ogden, Mormon Station, all the smaller Mormon settlements are walled due to attacks."

And it wasn't just the Utes on the warpath, Fargo knew. Roaming Apaches, too, were a threat. They'd been terrorizing the New Mexico Territory, bringing mining to a halt. Bannocks, too, were burning stagecoach stations in Utah and the goldfields of Oregon Territory.

"Most of the braves I've spotted," Fargo added, "are wearing wampum beads. That usually means heap big doin's."

For a moment John Beckmann's dirty, sweat-streaked face brightened. "Do you mean . . . a ceremony of some sort?"

Fargo struggled to be patient. "Yeah, if that's what you call greasing for war."

The pretty, petite brunette had edged closer. She flashed Fargo a smile full of gleaming white teeth. Her puffy, heart-shaped lips were a little moist now—as if inviting a kiss.

"John is a bachelor of arts," she explained. "A teacher. Means to start up a vocational school for Indians out in Los Angeles."

"Los Angeles? It's still more of a flyspeck on the map than a settlement, just a dusty little pueblo. But sometimes it's good to get in early."

"The aboriginals may kill us before we ever see it," Beckmann fretted, glancing at his children. "Don't the army outposts keep them in line?"

"There's Fort Bridger," Fargo replied, "but it's always undermanned. Dysentery keeps half the soldiers laid up. Did I say soldiers? Mostly it's a bunch of boys with their pants tucked into their boots. They send out patrols, but this is a lot of territory."

Fargo glanced at the exhausted party, especially the children and Estelline. She looked to be alarmingly close to her lying-in, and in her present exhausted condition desert travails could well kill her.

John Beckmann was a good man, Fargo concluded, and he admired the man's idealism if not his common sense. But clearly the shock of this rugged Far West frontier was too much for the man. They needed help, and Fargo had a few good friends here in Deseret, the original Mormon name for the Utah Territory settled by Latter-day Saints under Brigham Young.

"I'll give it to you with the bark still on it," Fargo said. "You won't make it. No water, no food, no money, no team or conveyance, nothing but the clothes on your back. And your wife, Mr. Beckmann, shouldn't be on a desert trail in her condition."

"Agreed, Mr. Fargo. But where can we go? Obviously I can't even locate my own shadow. I'm out of my element in the wilderness."

"Just like I'd be," Fargo reminded him, "in front of a classroom. For right now we'll work our way east around the northern tip of Great Salt Lake. There's a settlement called Mormon Station where we can stock up on water and supplies, maybe even get you folks a conveyance. Then we'll work our way south to Salt Lake City."

"Salt Lake City!" Dora exclaimed. "But you said it's far to the southeast."

"True, it's a long trek. But it's safe from Indian attack. Indians won't abide high casualties, so they've never become city fighters."

"But . . . it's all Latter-day Saints there, and we're Methodist! Won't they drive us out?"

Fargo shook his head. "The Saints are a bit clannish and suspicious of outlanders, especially those with the U.S. government. And some of the elders are openly hostile to non-Mormons. But they're mostly good, hard-working people and especially kind to travelers and children. They also need teachers and pay good wages to college men, so John could prob'ly earn your keep while you folks lay over, get back on your feet."

"It's a fine course of action, Mr. Fargo," Beckmann said. "But surely you must have other plans besides wet-nursing us?"

As a matter of fact Fargo had been heading out toward Pikes Peak to see if he, too, couldn't sell his services at the hugely inflated gold-camp rate. Prospectors were desperate for fresh meat, and good hunters could make a hundred dollars a day.

But Fargo watched Dora send him a low-lidded smile. *Hell*, he thought, *a man can profit in more ways than one.*

"After what just happened here," Fargo replied truthfully, "I'm a mite curious to hang around and poke along Dill Stover's back trail. This Childress fellow, too. There's too many poisoned water holes around here all of a sudden. And too many stirred-up Indians."

Fargo quickly erected a lean-to from his canvas ground sheet so the kids and Estelline could squeeze in out of the sun. Using Fargo's frying pan, and a fire pit against the wind, John Beckmann rustled up a quick meal of bacon and pan bread. At least, Fargo noted, the man was a good cook.

While Fargo examined the Ovaro's hoofs for stones and thorns, Dora studied him from a steady, curious gaze.

"Well, fella!" she exclaimed. "I didn't get a good size-up of you before. You're big enough to fight cougars with a shoe, are'n'cha?"

Fargo laughed at that one. "Sure, long as that shoe fires the right caliber bullet."

Boldly she reached out to squeeze his bicep. "My stars! You're built lanky, but you're hard as sacked salt!"

She stepped back to observe him critically. When she put her hands on her hips, Fargo watched her bodice stretch tight as a drumhead.

"A bit lean in the shanks," she finally noted. "That comes from living in the saddle. Have you ever settled down?"

"Nope. I'm just a westering wanderer," Fargo admitted. "Otherwise known as a drifter."

"And I'll just bet, drifter, the gals flock to you like flies to syrup, don't they?" she teased. "You're sinfully handsome."

Despite Dora's exhaustion, her big green eyes sparkled. Fargo realized she wasn't just pretty and well built—she also had brio *escondido*, "the hidden vigor." In a horse *or* a woman, this rare quality made for a more exciting ride.

"A gentleman never tells," Fargo told her with a smile.

"That's good to know," she replied. "I like to keep my . . . affairs private."

The playfulness melted from her face. "That man, Stover . . . what did you do to him? He's sure nursing a grudge."

"Some people, you don't need to *do* anything. Just my being alive chaps at Stover. He kept pushing until I had to slap him down a little."

"Did he mean that threat about killing you?" she pressed.

"It's no threat, he's already tried and will again. He has to because I mean to kill him. *What* in blazes are you doing, Dora?"

"This is my peeping stone. I bought it at a curio shop in St. Louis. Sometimes it shows me glimpses of the future. That's how I knew you were coming to save us."

Fargo felt a stab of disappointment as he watched the comely lass, back to the wind, stare intently into a ball of glass she pulled from the front pocket of her dress. All her flirting had got him all het up for some carnal fun with her later. Evidently, though, she was not quite right in her head.

"What do you see now?" he asked, humoring her.

"Just my own reflection," she admitted. "It doesn't always work. Sometimes—wait! There's something!"

14

Fargo, thumbing back his wet hat to see better, stared over her shoulder. "What? I don't see anything."

"It's . . . it's odd, Skye. I see neither you nor Dill Stover. But I see a . . . why, it's a calendar page! August tenth . . . and there's a window with a—a dawn sky behind it, I think. Oh, my stars! The picture's changing, Skye! I see a—a pretty young redheaded woman, and she's soaked in blood! Darn, now the peeping stone is empty."

"Hell, slyboots," Fargo scoffed. "There's no 'pictures' in that hunk of glass. This an act you're working up?"

She whirled toward him, eyes blazing. "You don't know sic 'em about such things! At daybreak on August tenth something terrible is going to happen. That's only about two weeks away."

"All right, where is all this going to happen?"

"I don't know," she admitted. "But I could've sworn I glimpsed a giant beehive for a second."

Fargo felt a little prickle of unease move along his spine. Couldn't Dora already have known that the beehive was the symbol of Deseret—and painted on an outer wall of the huge lecture hall in Salt Lake City? Constant labor, Brigham Young believed, was the key to happiness.

"Never mind," he said. "There's plenty of daylight left, we'll need to make tracks toward Mormon Station. With luck we'll reach it with only one camp in the desert."

"Suddenly," Dora told him, those heart-shaped lips smiling, "camping in this awful desert is an exciting prospect."

3

"Lately the desert seems to be crawling with grateful, thirsty customers, Cecil," remarked Frederic Lawton Childress. "This last trip out, I made four-hundred dollars on water alone. Not to mention the satisfied feeling that comes from helping one's fellow human beings."

Both men shared a laugh. Cecil McGinnis, editor and publisher of the *Desert Sentinel*, was a tall, balding, reed-thin man with a runneled forehead like creased leather. He filled two pony glasses with high-grade whiskey.

"Here's to the 'red menace' and noxious water," he proposed, clinking glasses with Childress. "May we prosper from both."

The men occupied a two-room cabin made of unbarked pine logs. It was McGinnis's home and the newspaper office. Tin lamp reflectors lined one wall, and a rusty stove sat on bricks, its firebox cold. Cool water in ollas, clay jars, was suspended from the roof beams.

It was midafternoon, about a day after Childress had encountered Skye Fargo and those destitute pilgrims in the desert southwest of Mormon Station. The northernmost of the Deseret settlements, Mormon Station was little more than a sizable cluster of cabins strung along an irrigation canal. Its large snowmelt reservoir explained the rye and wheat fields patterning the valley, where boys in wide-brimmed hats tended the communal herds.

"Not exactly a thriving metropolis with lyceums and opera houses," the newspaperman admitted, watching Childress gaze out the open door. "No tenpin alleys yet, Fred, as you'll find in Salt Lake City. But this is a self-sustaining community with carpenters, blacksmiths, gun-smiths, and shoemakers. We have a gristmill, weaving shops, a tannery, and storehouses."

Cecil's use of "we," Childress knew, was merely lip deep. McGinnis had eluded the law, back in Illinois, by pretending to convert to Mormonism and then joining an emigrant train bound for Deseret, now the Utah Territory. He continued pretending support for the religion as a cover for his criminal life.

"There's also a secret still in one of those storehouses," Childress reminded him. "And thanks to my progressive speeches about Indians, the Mormon High Council down in Salt Lake is convinced I'm a valuable citizen despite being an outlander. There may, however, be a new fly in the ointment, Cecil."

McGinnis, busy setting a tray of type for the next edition of his paper, glanced up. Alarm tightened his features. "How so?"

Childress quickly explained to his secret partner the encounter yesterday with Skye Fargo in the desert.

"Actually, I couldn't help admiring and even liking the fellow," Childress admitted. "Too bad we're going to have to kill him."

"I've been in the newspaper profession almost twenty years," McGinnis mused, frowning. "I've seen that name in several telegraphic dispatches over the years. Skye Fargo, the so-called Trailsman. Always being praised for dealing misery to criminals, though some claim *he's* a criminal."

Childress nodded, eyes thoughtful. He had bathed and changed into a suit. A gold watch and chain dangled across his fancy-stitched vest with its satin facings.

"Yes," he agreed, "Fargo carries the stink of a damned crusader. Just like this Captain Saunders Lee down in Salt Lake who wants to eliminate 'corruption.' If hot lead fails to silence Fargo, I might be needing your printing press to show the . . . less heroic side of this Trailsman to the Mormons."

"Hot lead?" McGinnis repeated. "Meaning you've already given the order to Dill Stover?"

"Order? Actually, no, which is even better. The moment I had the inventory safely locked in the storehouse, Stover headed back out into the desert. He and Fargo locked horns yesterday, and my guess is he means to bushwhack Fargo as he nears the settlement."

"*Bush*whack him? Fred, nothing grows on the Great Salt Desert."

"True, but it's not flat surface. A shallow swale will serve the purposes of a good marksman. And, for all his faults and disgusting habits, Stover *is* one hell of a marksman."

McGinnis conceded the point. Stover had won every major shooting competition in the territory. But his penchant for plugging Indians on sight had twice landed him in a Salt Lake City jail.

"Any luck," Childress asked, "with the Council's latest statehood petition?"

McGinnis shook his head. "Statehood was quick in California thanks to the Bear Flag Revolt. But Brigham's flagrant taking of yet another wife has some in the U.S. Congress raising Old Nick about it."

"Yes," Childress said, "no other territory has a history of federal officers storming off in protest as does Utah."

"Nothing bothers the pols as does polygamy," McGinnis insisted. "Remember how the 1856 platform of the Republican Party called Negro slavery, and polygamy in Utah, 'twin relics of barbarism'? They've even coined a word for plural-marriage homes out here: cohabs. Murder is nothing, our illegal grogshops hardly faze them. It's this plural-wives doctrine that will bring federal troops down on us any day now."

Childress scowled. "Agreed, damnit. Which is why we must profit as much, and as quickly, as possible. That means removing impediments like Skye Fargo so I can freely bleed the pilgrims. And continue to stir up the Utes—the Mormon Battalion is long overdue for rearming, and *we* have five-hundred new repeating rifles still packed in gun grease."

"There's another source of profit," the newspaperman reminded his partner, "that might survive federal takeover of Deseret."

Childress grinned. "That whopping contract the Mormons are offering for a mail-express service, right?"

"Right as rain. A sweet, juicy plum to whoever wins the Salt Lake Run. The last service in this area charged one

18

dollar a letter. A man could charge half that and still get rich."

"Or charge twice that," Childress said, "and get even richer. Don't worry, we'll have Stover in the race. And our Ute friends He Bear and Nothing but Trouble will be keeping an eye on the finish line to make sure Dill wins."

McGinnis suddenly thought of something. "Say! The Mormons advertise a big race, Fargo shows up—*he* won't be in this race next week, will he?"

"Judging from the determined look on Stover's face as he rode out," Childress replied, "and the quality of his sharp-shooting rifle, I'd guess no. Fargo won't be in the race next week. In fact, he won't even *be*."

Fargo cursed, but without heat.

At his first confused glance in the swirling desert glare, he had thought he was looking at a giant porcupine. But the "quills" were in fact a profusion of arrows with Ute clan markings. The dead man from which they protruded had died with agony etched deep into his features.

"Poor fellow was already dying of thirst when the Utes found him," Fargo told John Beckmann. "No papers on him, and no way in hell we can bury him out here—it's *borrasca* beneath that salt dust. We'll heap some stones over him and report it in Mormon Station."

It was around noon of the day following the tense encounter with Stover and Childress. The two youngest Beckmann children, four-year-old Lloyd and six-year-old Sarah, were taking their turns in the Ovaro's saddle. They had been switching off with Frank and Katy, who were eight and ten. The expecting Estelline, too, was given regular turns on horseback. The other three adults walked without relief except for short breaks to rest the tired Ovaro.

"Why was he killed, Skye?" Dora asked, averting her eyes from the body to glance nervously around. "Looks like he had nothing."

"Indians rarely kill a man just to rob him," Fargo said. "This is about territory, not robbery. That body is meant to scare other white men out of the region. I've seen others like it since I left the Humboldt River country west of here, some scalped, some—"

Fargo realized the older children were listening.

19

"Anyway, all the more reason," he concluded, "to get you folks to Salt Lake City and some shelter."

Fargo considered it nothing short of amazing that the Beckmann party had escaped Indian scrapes this long, especially with someone in this area stirring up the pot by selling liquor and guns to the Utes. Or so the U.S. Cavalry believed, and Fargo had seen the signs, too.

For that matter, he himself had been lucky so far. Fargo's last skirmish with Indians had been in the Mescal Mountains east of here, when a renegade group of outlaw Apaches had ambushed him at the head of aptly named Disappointment Creek. Fortunately, they carried only single-shot dragoon pistols, and the repeating Henry with its tubular magazine held sixteen shots.

Dora, who made Fargo nervous with her "peeping stone," seemed to read his thoughts now.

"Will they attack us, too?" she asked. "I've . . . I've heard what they do to women."

"Five hours or so," Fargo reminded her, "we'll be in Mormon Station. It's walled and has bastions with sentries."

Food, water, and a few hours sleep had done wonders for the stranded party. With John Beckmann's energetic help Fargo soon covered the dead man. While they worked, Fargo gazed carefully in every direction, watching for dust puffs, reflections, any signs of danger.

This salt-encrusted desert contained none of the vegetation of the Arizona and New Mexico deserts—no flowering mescal, no white-plumed Spanish bayonet, no mesquite pods. And the bone-dry mountains surrounding them were without the usual shadowed pockets of snow higher up. *No question about it,* Fargo thought. *Some of the most harrowing deserts of the intermountain West began here west of Salt Lake.* And he was caught smack in the middle of one now like a gobbet of flesh in a giant frying pan.

"Why would the Mormons even *want* this wasteland?" John burst out, eyes watering from the burning glare and blowing grit.

"Settling in this area was a stroke of genius, not ignorance," Fargo assured him as the party started forward again. "The Mormons were being driven out and killed back east. Brigham Young knew the Saints needed a homeland too harsh to be coveted by outsiders. So he selected the bone-dry stretch between the Wasatch Range and the Great Salt Lake. All it needed was irrigation from the mountains."

"But *that*," Beckmann said, pointing back at the stone-covered body. "Have the Mormons angered the Indians somehow? I've read that the Latter-day Saints hold progressive views about the Indians, whom they call Lamanites and consider one of the Ten Lost Tribes of Israel. In fact, their enlightened attitude helped shape my desire to start a school for Indians."

Fargo shook his head. "Mormons get along all right with the tribes. They decided early on its cheaper to feed Indians than to fight them. Only problem came when the Utah Territorial government made it illegal to sell captured children to the Comancheros, slave-traders in New Mexico Territory. The Ute Indians, who are big slave-takers, rebelled. They started taking scalps, burning down mills. But the Mormons wore them down with patience. No, whatever or whoever has set the tribes off lately is doing it deliberately."

"To what purpose?" Dora asked. She walked beside Fargo, on the side giving a little shade.

"Most likely profit," Fargo replied promptly, recalling yesterday's encounter with Childress. " 'Indian threats' can be a bonanza for some."

Fargo glanced down at Dora's bare feet. "Sure you don't want me to wrap them?"

"No point to it now. The soles of my feet are so leather tough you could strike a match on them."

She lowered her voice and added, "But I'm soft in all the important places."

Much to Fargo's regret, sick and crying kids, as well as bone-deep exhaustion, had quelled any romantic impulses last night.

Fargo glanced back at the others. They, too, were all barefoot.

"First we boiled hides and bones for food," Dora explained. "Then we ate our belts and footgear."

"Tastes like crap," volunteered ten-year-old Katy.

"Don't I know," Fargo told the kid. "I boiled my buckskins once."

John Beckmann had saved an old mule-ear Kentucky rifle that seemed in good repair. It was slung across his back.

"Got loads for that?" Fargo asked.

Beckmann's sunburned face nodded. "I've never shot at a man, but I've done plenty of hunting for game. I'm a fair marksman, given time to aim."

"That's fine," Fargo said, "if white devils jump us. But Indians never give a man time to aim. You have to get good at snap-shooting. A glimpse is all you'll see, if that."

"So you do think we'll be attacked?"

Fargo lifted a shoulder. "After Mormon Station, we still have to travel south to Salt Lake, so yeah—distinct possibility. If not by Indians, then by Dill Stover. But he'll be after me, not you folks."

"Is he as vicious as he seems?" Estelline asked. She leaned against her husband for support as they trudged across the alkali wasteland.

"He's poison mean," Fargo assured her. "And low. He'd steal the coppers from a dead man's eyes."

Fargo knew it wasn't just the fact that he'd publicly whipped Stover's ass. Until Fargo's arrival at Mary's Station, Stover had made his brag that he was a "scout and tracker." He failed miserably at both, and it was all the more obvious once Fargo showed up. The men had tormented Stover mercilessly when he was demoted to mule packer. Now he acted like Fargo had stolen his laurels.

"Poison mean," Dora repeated. "Well, you sure don't act like a man who recently faced down two guns and has a death threat hanging over him. Is that a *grin* on your handsome face?"

It was, and now it stretched wider. For Fargo, death was as real as a man beside him—a man who never went away. But the Trailsman was damned if he'd let that fact ruin his cheerful disposition.

Still, Fargo was no fool who ignored danger. Stover's recent words snapped in memory like burning twigs: *Next time I'll kill you.*

After another slug of corpse-reviver (Irish poteen, the area's strongest bootleg liquor except for Indian burner), Dill Stover was by-god *ready*.

He swung down from his roan gelding and buried the picket pin in the sand. He had selected the tallest of a series of sandstone rises west of Mormon Station. Anyone approaching the settlement from the desert to the west would pass this spot. The northeast shoulder of Great Salt Lake was visible, so sparkling bright Stover couldn't glance at it more than a few seconds.

The latest sandstorm had cut visibility to ten yards. But now the wind had abated. And soon Fargo and his pathetic human strays should be in view.

"All right, Fargo," Stover said softly as he untied a buckskin rifle sheath from his cantle straps, "it's time to kiss the mistress."

With loving care he removed a Sharps Big Fifty equipped with a fancy German scope. The weapon fired 700-grain slugs that could easily drop an adult buffalo from a mile off.

Stover walked to the rocky edge of the rise, eyes searching the vast, almost surreal openness. Heat pockets shimmered, and the eyes played optical tricks on a man. Spotting one man, out here, was like trying to find a sliver in an elephant's ass.

But Stover had the vision of an eagle, and though he wasn't a "quick draw" expert, he had few peers as a target shooter. His eyes went dark with brooding as Skye Fargo filled the screen of his mind.

Oh, Christ, Stover knew that sneaky type, all right. Men like Fargo pretended to be the quiet, modest joes. But in truth Fargo was one of those boasters just bursting at the seams to talk himself up mighty high while doing all he could to humiliate his betters.

Stover stroked the long barrel of the Big Fifty.

"One little kiss," he muttered, "and Fargo takes a long nap."

Stover settled in behind the rocks, patiently waiting.

4

"Those sandstone rises dead ahead," Fargo said, pointing through the swirling white alkali dust, "mark the western boundary of Mormon Station. We should make the settlement before dark."

Fargo carried his Henry with a square of rawhide tied over the muzzle as a dustcover. His face, like that of his seven charges, was a white mask with dirty streaks from sweating. The white hair and beard aged him twenty years.

"How did you ever find it?" John Beckmann marveled. "There weren't even any landmarks to guide you."

"I had to work out the route last night while there were stars," Fargo admitted.

In this vast, featureless terrain he had been forced to wait for nightfall. Then, relying on the Pole Star and the Dog Star as reference points, he literally drew an arrow in the sand to point them off the next morning.

Right now, however, Fargo didn't like the location of those rises. He'd forgotten how commanding they were. Even if a scum bucket named Dill Stover hadn't threatened his life yesterday, Fargo would rather swing wide of such a natural ambush point. But the Great Salt Lake, on his right, and an impassable expanse of sand dunes to the left, served to funnel travelers into a narrow trough beside the sandstone rises.

"Something wrong?" Dora asked. Those pretty, wing-shaped eyes studied him anxiously.

"If there is," Fargo assured her, "we can handle it."

It amazed him that a woman could still look so damn fetching after days of near-starvation and wandering in a brutal desert.

"No, I require a bath right now," her voice surprised him

as if he'd spoken. "You ought to see me in a hoopskirt and a fancy two-story bonnet. You might also like me in a chemise."

Fargo's bearded jaw dropped in astonishment. "But I didn't say a word. How'd you know what I was thinking?"

"Same way I see pictures in my peeping stone—it just happens sometimes. Don't ask me how."

Fargo, still skeptical but intrigued, said, "So you're saying you *really* see . . . pictures in that glass?"

"Sometimes I can. And most times when I do, it gives me belly flies. When I was a little girl, I used to have—well, spells, sort of. Trances."

"It's true, Mr. Fargo," Estelline called over. "About the spells, I mean. One day when she was twelve, Dora suddenly announced that our Uncle Roderick wouldn't be coming home ever again. Three days later we received a message saying he was killed in a barge accident on the Erie Canal."

Fargo's hands were full just dealing with the natural world, and he'd found little time or interest for things supernatural. Still . . . it was unsettling that Dora claimed to have seen a beehive in her bloody, terrifying vision, a symbol found all over Salt Lake City. Deseret, the old name for Utah Territory, was the Mormon word for honeybee.

Supposedly, August tenth, at daybreak, was the time that Dora's prediction would come true. She had a calendar and said that was fourteen days away.

Fargo glanced around to see how everyone was holding up. The two youngest kids, Lloyd and Sarah, were tied to the saddle of the Ovaro. Both of them nodded in and out of sleep. Frank and Katy were trudging along like little troopers, and John and Dora, too, were holding up—in John's case, by will alone. But Estelline truly worried Fargo.

She was plucky and sweet, but, like her college-educated husband, completely out of her element here. Los Angeles they might survive if that backward hamlet solved its water-shortage problem. But a frail, exhausted woman like Estelline could never survive giving birth in the arid, burning desert hell that was only beginning.

"Let's spell my horse," Fargo called, mainly to give Estelline a rest.

While everyone took a breather in the meager shade of some black volcanic rocks, Fargo carefully examined his cinches, latigos, stirrups, halter, and reins. He cut a few fringes from his buckskin shirt and used them to mend a weak spot in one of the cinches. Then he once again checked the Ovaro's hoofs for cracks or lodged stones.

"It's been rough sledding, old campaigner," Fargo said, scratching the stallion's withers. "Soon's you tote these tads to Mormon Station, you're getting a roomy stall, clean straw, and a nosebag of crushed barley."

Dora sat on a nearby pile of rocks to watch him.

"You surely do pay attention to details when it comes to that horse," she teased in a low tone. "You that . . . thorough with women, too?"

Fargo grinned and opened his mouth to reply. But just then he saw it, straight behind and well above Dora's head: a winking flash of light. Something on that first rise, reflecting sunlight.

Maybe something like Dill Stover's silver-trimmed vaquero saddle.

"Rock piles," he told Dora casually, "are favorite haunts of rattlesnakes."

She quickly scooted off. Again, as Fargo eased between her and the sandstone rise, he was impressed by her wasp-waisted figure and slim, nicely turned ankles.

"How in hell can a gal as comely as you still be unhitched?" Fargo asked, though his eyes flicked to all sides and, especially, overhead.

"Oh, I've had plenty of chances. My parents both died of cholera when I was eighteen, and the proposals started rolling in. The most recent was from a nice fellow in Kentucky. But I'm not the type to grub taters on some back-hill farm."

She pursed those puffy, moist, heart-shaped lips, making Fargo's own lips itch to kiss them into submission.

"Sometimes, when a girl likes men *too* much," she added, "she simply can't limit herself to just one of them, you know? Marriage, to me, is like going out to dinner all your life, but only being allowed to order the same item every night. Even a favorite meal gets boring."

Fargo's strong white teeth flashed through his beard. "Well, that's a page from my own book."

But as they resumed the journey, Fargo couldn't get that reflection just now, atop the rise, out of his mind. It didn't "belong to the place" as one old tracker used to tell him. Nor did the poisoned water. The clues were abundant: seeing vast opportunity and little law, Dill Stover's employers, Childress and no doubt others, had quite possibly formed a criminal ring, much like the ones that thrived in lawless 1840s San Francisco.

Just then they cleared a long, sloping ridge, and even the two older children exclaimed at their first sight of astounding Salt Lake Valley. It was shaped like a giant amphitheater and ringed completely by mountains. Thanks to irrigation it was brilliant with green grass, and large fields of cucumbers, melons, and squash, separated by grape-stake fences. Fargo spotted cattle, hogs, chickens, turkeys, all of excellent quality. Broad-leaved cottonwoods and tall poplars, while not profuse, were a welcome sight after the arid and featureless salt desert.

"Why, the place is thriving!" John exclaimed.

"Yeah, these folks don't need clocks," Fargo said. "The workday goes on from can to can't. Only way to whip a desert into submission."

Another brief wink of light from atop that distant rise, and this time Fargo felt the all-too-familiar "goose tickle" in the back of his neck.

He untied Sarah from the saddle, then Lloyd. He handed Sarah to her father, Lloyd to Dora.

"My turn to ride now," he told the curious adults as he lengthened the stirrups.

If that was Dill Stover up there, Fargo sure's hell didn't want him confused on his targets. It was a long way off—at least six hundred yards. Fargo meant to ride out in front.

The Trailsman swung up onto the hurricane deck. *Let the yellow-bellied dry-gulcher take his best shot. He'd better make it a damn good one,* Fargo thought, *because eventually I'll get my turn, too.*

During Dill Stover's long wait the sandstorms had kicked up again, and he had cursed with violent rage at the prospect of losing this chance to shoot an air shaft through Fargo.

But finally Lady Luck apparently had a crush on him,

Stover decided. A bubble of elation rose within him as he watched that crusading bastard Skye Fargo mount his stallion and ride out ahead of the others. Real *noble*. Also real convenient for Stover.

"It's money for old rope," he gloated as he settled the butt plate of his scope-equipped Sharps Big Fifty into his shoulder socket.

He sprawled out in a prone position at the very lip of the sandstone formation, hidden by a low rock parapet. Stover inhaled a long breath, expelled it slowly while he relaxed his entire body. His trigger finger took up the slack in one long, continuous pull.

But he stopped on the feather edge of actually firing, wanting to let Fargo come even closer. Stover knew this had to be a clean, one-shot kill. Fargo wasn't the type to panic and freeze in place while a man reloaded.

"Yeah, just keep on coming, big man," Stover muttered, watching Fargo grow larger in the German-made scope. "It'll be quick."

Fargo glanced back to check on the others and was just in time for a little skin show. With plenty of water now well in sight, he had relaxed the rationing rules somewhat. And Dora, seeing him look back from the saddle, chose that moment to unbutton her shirtwaist and sponge off her "neck."

Because of the heat she had skipped the usual layers of undergarments. Fargo enjoyed a loin-stirring glimpse of creamy white breasts and plum-colored nipples.

"Dora," Estelline called out in a kind, gently reproving voice, "I don't mind Mr. Fargo looking at you. But my John is sneaking peeks, too."

"What red-blooded man wouldn't be?" Fargo muttered to himself.

But that first sandstone rise, now looming larger against the afternoon sky, reminded Fargo of his duty.

Yet, danger seemed remote. The sky had cleared to a deep, gas-flame blue, and a glance to the right showed peaceful life in the Salt Lake Valley. Purple-hazed mountains marched along distant horizons. Davy Crockett, Fargo recalled idly, once had a trading post out this way.

Just for a heartbeat, reflected light winked from up above on the rise.

"Here's the fandango!" Fargo told the Ovaro, even as he jerked his feet from the stirrups.

"Everybody *down*!" he roared to those behind him. "Grown-ups cover the kids!"

Fargo snatched his Henry from its boot and jacked a round into the chamber. He rolled off the Ovaro only a fractional second before a big gun spoke its piece from overhead.

Jesus! Fargo flinched at the concussive, ear-splitting crack. The bullet nicked the bow of his saddle, then sent up a pluming geyser of salt dust when it punched into the desert floor. Fargo grabbed the bridle and wheeled the Ovaro back toward the others, slapping his glossy rump.

All this took only seconds, and there was still a blue feather of telltale powder smoke hovering up above, marking the shooter's position. Fargo, taking up a kneeling off-hand position, dropped the Henry's front sight on that parapet of rock above. He peppered it with eight quick shots, sending rock dust and chips spraying everywhere.

He paused to learn the ambusher's next move. A second shot, from a new position above. A child screamed behind Fargo, and fear licked at his belly.

He cursed, face twisted with anger, and emptied the rest of his magazine on this new position.

"It's all right, everybody," Dora called out, her voice tense and trembling with fear. "The second bullet hit close, it scared Lloyd, is all."

Might have been a ranging shot, Fargo thought. *If so, the third bullet,* he realized in an anxious fret, *might well hit one of those kids. And in a few seconds the shooter will be loaded again.*

Fargo, intently focused on the sandstone rise, had paid scant attention to the east, where the sky had begun ominously, mysteriously darkening.

"Look! Good heart of God, *look*!"

John Beckmann was so agitated that his Adam's apple bobbed up and down each time he spoke. He pointed east toward the valley, so astounded at what he saw that even the shooter was momentarily forgotten.

Fargo's eyes followed John's finger.

"Well, I'm a Dutchman," Fargo muttered, awed and horrified by the disaster now descending.

Stover was taking up the trigger slack for his next shot when the light dimmed as if it were an eclipse.

He glanced east, then felt his blood turn to ice. The daytime sky had gone black out over the valley.

"Crickets!"

A voracious black cloud of them descended on the barley, wheat, and alfalfa fields. They made the air hum and screech. At Dill's present altitude, plenty of the insects were smacking into his face, too.

Stover swore, unable to get a good shot off with frenzied crickets gnawing his clothing. And only a fool would hang around up here very long when Skye Fargo was after him.

"We'll lock horns, big man," Stover promised. Then he sheathed his Big Fifty and pulled out the roan's picket pin.

Fargo knew, from the dust puffs, exactly when the ambusher left. But he had no plans to follow him. He had a good lead, and if it was Dill Stover, a good horse. Fargo would get nothing but his dust.

Instead, he slogged upward toward a ridge overlooking the valley. He crested it and immediately felt his stomach sink. The fields below were covered with a shifting black blanket of ravenous crickets.

But at the very moment Fargo topped the ridge, there was a massive stirring sound to his right. Thousands of gulls covered Great Salt Lake. As if Fargo's arrival were a signal, they rose en masse, descended on the crickets, and began devouring them without injuring the crops.

Cheers and shouts erupted from the farmers below, and several were pointing up at Fargo.

"Oh, hell," he muttered to himself, "do I have to be a *hero* again?"

5

"What in the world?" Dora said, staring at a huge broadsheet plastered to the baked-mud wall surrounding Mormon Station.

The gulls had returned to the lake, their unexpected meal finished, by the time Fargo's group trudged the last few miles. Now the tired, salt-encrusted party halted to read the broadsheet:

> MORMON MEN, ARM YOURSELVES WITH MODERN WEAPONS!!
> THE "SCABS OF MANKIND" THREATEN YOUR HOMELAND!! IN
> ONE WESTERN COUNTY OF ONLY 600 SOULS, 100 HAVE BEEN
> MURDERED OUTRIGHT BY SAVAGES! NOT TO MENTION THE
> HORRIBLE MUTILATIONS, THE CHILDREN TAKEN CAPTIVE,
> THE WOMEN WHO ARE "OUTRAGED" (TO PUT IT DELI-
> CATELY). THE GENTILE GOVERNMENT IN WASHINGTON CITY
> DOESN'T GIVE A TINKER'S DAMN ABOUT OUR SAFETY! WE
> MUST PADDLE FOR OURSELVES!!

"Gentile?" Dora said, puzzled. "Did Jewish people write this?"

"No, that's what Mormons call anyone outside their religion, Jews included," John Beckmann explained. He turned questioning eyes toward Fargo.

"I don't understand this poster," he said. "I thought the Latter-day Saints have good relations with the Indians?"

"That broadsheet wasn't authorized, I'd wager," Fargo said, thinking of the ambush from the sandstone rises—he had a hunch the two were related. "No proof Mormons even put it up. I suspect it's being done at night—see where a bunch of them have been whitewashed over?"

"What's it say, Mr. Fargo?" demanded Katy, the oldest of the four kids.

"What's it *say*? Why, hon, walls can't talk."

Fargo made a goofy face and tickled Katy. She cried out in laughing, wiggling torment and forgot about her question.

They continued on toward the main gate of the settlement, which remained open during daylight hours. The dust-powdered Ovaro, more white than black, whinnied as he scented the sweet-smelling clover and alfalfa.

Fargo glanced out at the unwalled part of the northern Salt Lake Valley, watching the men return to working their fields after the near disaster. Even their harshest critics praised the Mormons for their work ethic. Some of these in the fields were among the "handcart Mormons." Being driven from their homes back east and facing a wagon shortage, they pushed their belongings cross country to Deseret in wooden handcarts, a hellish undertaking many did not survive.

"My stars!" Dora exclaimed as they stepped through the log gate and past a twelve-pound howitzer. "Is this a reception committee or a lynch mob?"

Fargo felt his gorge rise when he saw the knot of men hurrying toward the new arrivals. Those smiles wreathing their faces meant he was now at the center of attention— one place he hated to be because lead tended to fly there.

"Skye Fargo!" called out Abraham Winslowe, a Mormon elder Fargo recognized from Salt Lake City. "Timely met, Trailsman! Perhaps you've done it again, young fellow. God bless you."

"Done what again?" Dora muttered, unnerved by all the male eyes now studying her—a few with harsh disapproval. "They all seem to know you."

In fact, for some time Fargo had been in good standing with the Mormon community. The High Council in Salt Lake City had hired him, a few years back, when the settlers on the southern border suffered devastating crop failures.

In Parowan, Washington, and Cedar City floods washed away dams and good soil. Folks needed resupply in a serious hurry, and Fargo, the Mormon Battalion right behind him, had blazed a relief trail through sixty miles of interconnecting canyons. They were just in time: the residents were all bones with faces tinted blue from starvation.

"This display a bit ago with the gulls was miraculous," exclaimed a reedy, furrow-browed man with printer's ink on his knuckles. He extended his hand. "Cecil McGinnis, editor of the local newspaper."

"I'm not so quick to call it a miracle," Elder Winslowe chimed in, frowning through his full gray beard at McGinnis. "But I will concede: the very moment Skye appeared on the ridge, the gulls rose up. And it appears there is very little damage to our crops. At a minimum it's God's grace."

Fargo surprised them by replying matter-of-factly, "Any of you gents seen Dill Stover around today?"

"Stover? I hear he's enlisted in the U.S. Army," McGinnis answered quickly.

"Why, I saw him this very day," Elder Winslowe gainsaid. "He rode in earlier this afternoon with Fred Childress, then rode out again by himself."

"Toward the sandstone rises west of here?" Fargo pressed.

"In that direction, yes."

Still no proof, Fargo thought. *But it will turn out to be Stover, sure as cats fighting.*

Fargo quickly introduced the elder and his companions to the seven destitute travelers, explaining their dilemma.

Elder Winslowe cast a sympathetic eye on the weary, dirty children and Estelline, who leaned on her husband for support.

"Our bounty is to be shared. Yes, take them to Salt Lake City for the birthing," Winslowe agreed. "In fact, I am going back there myself tomorrow and have a good team of oxen and a large wagon. Also, I can hire Mr. Beckmann right now to teach Latin at City Creek School, assuming he agrees to avoid any disrespect to Brigham Young and our creed. The position pays seventy-five dollars a month in U.S. money."

That was twice what teachers back East were paid. Beckmann, all smiles, gratefully accepted. The Mormons conferred among themselves quickly, then a farmer in a blue work uniform led the new arrivals through the orderly settlement.

Dogs were everywhere, kept for security against Indians. No saloons here, Fargo recalled regretfully. No green-baize poker tables, no soiled doves selling their favors in rickety cribs. He glanced at Dora and she pouted—the best good time in town? He hoped to find out later.

Their guide took them to a plain but comfortable house near an irrigation ditch at the rear of the settlement, just inside the wall. The Mormon family who once lived there, their guide explained, was ordered to resettle in San Bernardino, California. Now the home was kept for transients.

"You can see where it started as a single-room mud hut," Beckmann remarked when the farmer had left. "But part of the original walls seems to have crumbled."

"In a hard rain," Fargo explained, "baked-mud buildings will dissolve."

That original mud hut had been expanded to a clapboard structure with six rooms. A solid floor of split slab had been polished in the usual manner by covering it with ground corn, then holding a dance. Out back were a barn, stable, coops, and outbuildings.

Fargo ended up with one of the three bedrooms to himself, a neat cubbyhole with a single sash window and a threadbare, rose-patterned carpet. A goose-down mattress covered the narrow iron bedstead.

Nor would he need to seek out a livery and pay the exorbitant rates charged to emigrants along the California Trail. There was a paddock and abundant grass out back, a stack of new hay, and the irrigation ditch was filled with clean mountain water. Fargo stripped the rigging off his Ovaro, then rubbed him down good with a dry feed sack and turned him out into the paddock, pitching in some hay.

A stick snapped behind him.

Fargo ducked and whirled, though he stopped his hand before his Colt cleared leather.

"Skye!" Dora protested.

"Well, Jesus, lady. Don't sneak up on a fella with all the enemies I've got."

"I have to sleep with Sarah," the petite brunette protested, so angry she looked on the verge of stamping her foot. "And I'd have to sneak through John and Estelline's room to get to you. John wakes up at a cough. This'll be two nights in a row that we can't . . . you know, get together."

Fargo grinned. "Where there's a will . . . you got a window in your room?"

She nodded.

"So do I. Look at that grassy, rolling bank beside the ditch. And all those cedars forming a screen. Won't nobody see us back here except my stallion, and he's no gossip."

Dora's pretty face brightened. "Meet you under the stars?"

"With the bit in my teeth," he assured her. "I'll tap on your window."

"When?"

"Hard to say," Fargo hedged. "I've got something to do first."

"Skye?"

"Hmm?"

"I'm worried about going down to Salt Lake City. I mean, those Mormons just now seemed awfully nice to us. But is it just because they like you?"

"Gentiles can get by in Utah," he replied. "But they don't generally thrive. Still, you folks only need to stay until Estelline has her baby."

"About two months. And a couple more while it gets strong enough to travel," Dora said.

"Just remember, it doesn't matter whether you're a Saint or an outlander. *Everybody* in Deseret, no exceptions, has to watch out for Brigham Young, the Elders, and the Church."

"But you said Mr. Childress is a gentile, and he seems to be thriving."

Fargo nodded. A line from that broadsheet leaped out from memory: MORMON MEN, ARM YOURSELVES WITH MODERN WEAPONS!!

"He sure does seem to be thriving," Fargo agreed. "I mean to shake that tree a little, see what falls out."

He heard tug chains jingling as the short-line stage to Logan and Brigham rattled past the settlement, not bothering to stop since the passenger flag wasn't flying from the gate.

Dora seemed to recall something. "You remember what I saw in my peeping stone?"

Fargo nodded as he picked up his saddle.

"That beehive I saw," she hurried on. "You didn't say anything when I mentioned it. But I saw one on the wall by the gate. I asked John, and he said it's the symbol of Deseret. You knew that, didn't you?"

"I s'pose I did," Fargo admitted.

"And the calendar page I saw in my peeping stone, the one that read August tenth," she reminded him. "The woman drenched in blood. Those images mean nothing to you?"

" 'Fraid not."

Fargo didn't want to insult her, but she could easily be trying to bamboozle him, perhaps just to make herself look important. He had no proof she'd never heard of Deseret's symbol. It wouldn't be that hard to learn.

"August tenth," she repeated. "That's only two weeks from now."

He ignored her and crossed to a gun port in the wall, glancing west. The setting sun was a dull orange ball balanced just above the horizon. Serrated mountains, purple-black in the fading light, filled the far distance. Just beyond the irrigated fields, the slopes bristled with dusty clumps of sage.

"Salt Lake City has some life after dark," he said, "but these border settlements roll up early. I'm gonna wash up quick, then go visit with the men, find out a little more about Childress. This fellow McGinnis interests me, too."

"Why?"

"He's got a printing press, that's why," Fargo replied, thinking of that broadsheet. "Not too many of those out here yet."

"I'll be waiting for your knock on my window," Dora called behind him. "With baited breath."

Fargo left his saddle and Henry in his room, washed up at the bucket out back, then followed a dirt path out front toward the heart of the settlement. Outside the high walls, the last bloodred rays of sun still gold-leafed the sage; within, it was that indeterminate, grainy time of evening "between dog and wolf."

Dill Stover was on the loose. So Fargo palmed the butt of his Colt when several shadowy forms neared him.

"Gunman," a disapproving voice said as the men passed him. "Another godless gentile."

"Pure pagan and proud of it, boys," Fargo called out cheerfully. "Give my love to your wives and daughters."

A knot of men had gathered outside a blacksmith shop. Fargo lingered in the lengthening shadows, listening to them.

"They sign the peace treaties just to get the presents," carped a man dressed like a clerk.

"God's truth," agreed a farmer. "We feed them all winter just so we can fight them all summer."

A murmur of assent rolled through the men. *Whoever is behind creating the local "red menace,"* Fargo thought, *is doing a pretty good job of it.*

He moved on, seeking out Childress. Two men were smoking under a lantern that hung over the porch stoop of a log dwelling. A painted sign over the door read THE DESERT SENTINEL. Frederic Childress and Cecil McGinnis, Fargo realized as he angled toward the two men.

"Skye Fargo!" McGinnis exclaimed, glad-handing him as did Childress. "We were just talking about you. What with all the Ute uprising lately, it's a comfort to have a man of your reputation with us."

"Matter of fact," Childress tossed in, "we were discussing a salary offer if you'd agree to live here."

"Thank you kindly, gents. But I won't live anyplace where I have to pay tax on the meat I shoot. And in Utah it's taxed."

"That's as may be, Mr. Fargo," Childress replied, his gold watch chain gleaming in the lantern light. "But I don't pay Chinaman's wages. A few puny taxes won't matter."

"At fifteen dollars for a glass of water," Fargo said mildly, "I reckon you *can* pay generous wages."

"Well, folks are always free to ride to the eastern Utah outposts of Fort Bridger and Fort Supply if they don't like my terms."

That was hogwash, but Fargo decided not to push it. At the moment he wanted information, not confrontation.

"Dill Stover around?" he asked Childress.

"He's barred from the settlement after dark. Transient gentiles can overnight, but very few live here. Besides, he's a drunken sot and a bully. He spreads his lice-infected blankets out on the desert somewhere."

Fargo nodded. "These Indian troubles," he remarked, keeping his tone neutral, "always get worse when the white man sells them liquor. Liquor packing twice the powder load of white man's joy juice."

Both men nodded vigorously. Their faces looked angular and chiseled in the flickering light—at times, even sinister.

"Truer words and all that," Childress agreed. "But it's damnable work, finding these illegal grogshops. They can be dismantled with twenty minutes notice."

"I've never known an Indian to operate one," Fargo said. "It's always white men."

There was no accusation in his tone. But Fargo saw both men exchange the briefest of glances.

"From the red man's view of it," McGinnis said piously, broadening the subject in order to change it, "he's being told he has to trade buffalo for sheep. It's not a swap he favors, and I can't say that I blame him."

It sounded phony and put up, to Fargo. Hatchet-faced McGinnis had all the compassion of a cholera epidemic. Fargo decided to roll the dice and see if he could draw them out on their true feelings.

"No offense, gents," he replied. "I like the Mormon people just fine. But their sweet-lavender humility about Indians, all this brotherly love tripe, ain't my gait. Indians *are* the scabs of humanity, and that's straight arrow."

There was a long pause while Childress and McGinnis exchanged another look, reaching a decision.

"We appreciate your frankness, Mr. Fargo," Childress finally replied. "Let me also be candid. I don't hold with 'making palaver' with gut-eating savages who never even learned to harness the wheel. I say exterminate the lot of them. But Brother Brigham teaches that the 'Lamanites' have souls and all that swamp gas. So, as a gentile who wants to keep my merchant's license in Deseret, I must pare the cheese mighty close to the rind."

Fargo had decided his hunch was right. It was almost surely the printing press, visible now behind McGinnis's tall, thin frame, that was producing those anti-Indian screeds and increasing the bloodshed. The remote settlements always strayed from the dogma and laws set forth in

Salt Lake City. Especially when cold, calculating criminals were in the mix. Fargo wasn't sure about McGinnis. But Childress, despite his satin facings and senate-chamber speaking style, was not only crooked but tough as a wolverine.

"Any chance you'll change your mind about that job?" Childress asked.

"A slight chance," Fargo lied.

"That pinto stallion you led in earlier," Childress said, "was dusty and bottomed out. But that's some first-rate horseflesh. Why don't you enter him in the Salt Lake Run?"

"That stallion could turn on a two-bit piece and give you back fifteen cents in change," Fargo boasted. "But those are go muscles, not show muscles."

"Show?" McGinnis exclaimed. "Mr. Fargo, this race is not a cowboy contest for bragging rights. Besides two hundred and fifty dollars, the winner receives a lucrative contract to operate an express-mail service between Salt Lake and San Bernardino. A man can clear a thousand a month."

Fargo shook his head. "My horse isn't just a possession, Mr. McGinnis. He's an old trail companion. I save his vinegar for tight scrapes, not got-up races."

Fargo wanted them convinced he wasn't interested. But in fact he was starting to rethink this race coming up in Salt Lake City. To hell with the mail contract—the race itself just might fit into his plans perfectly.

After all, he'd likely be in Salt Lake City soon, anyway. So would Childress, and perhaps Dill Stover with him. Fargo had some serious questions that somebody *was* by God going to answer. All the way across the grueling salt flats, Fargo had encountered deliberately poisoned water holes. First had come the dead stock, then the shallow human graves, then the exposed bodies of those with no one left to cover them.

Fargo meant to find out who caused that grisly trail of death. And if he could make a little money at the same time—say, two hundred and fifty dollars for winning that race—all the better.

"Well, sleep tight, gents," he told the two men.

They watched his tall shape blend into the inky fathoms of shadow.

39

"That bastard will train-wreck us," Childress muttered. "I just realized—he foxed us with that anti-Indian remark to draw us out."

McGinnis grunted assent. "I fell for it, too. *Why* did you bring up the race? We don't want him competing against Stover."

"You forget—a set course is the easiest place to ambush a man. But we can't wait for the race. Fargo is explosive trouble."

Something familiar in his partner's tone alerted McGinnis. He lowered his voice. "You mean . . . He Bear and Nothing but Trouble?"

Childress nodded. "I smuggled them in under the tarp of the buckboard. They're waiting in our storehouse. After it's done, they'll slip out the sally port. It's close to the house Fargo's in."

The sally port was a solid iron door in the wall, locked by a heavy wooden bar dropped into metal brackets.

"It's ideal," McGinnis gloated. "We not only rip a thorn from our sides by killing Fargo, but we visibly increase the Indian menace. Fargo was already a 'folk hero' to Mormons and gentiles alike. Now he'll be the bishops' pet after Salt Lake papers publish the 'miracle of the gulls,' which I telegraphed to them today. Perhaps the Indian slaughter of a popular gentile hero will even sway the Big Boss to change his tune and declare war."

"Maybe, maybe not," Childress said, his pale, slitted eyes still watching the spot where the night had absorbed Fargo. "But in a few hours Skye Fargo will be a side of meat, and *that's* the main mile."

6

Another hour passed, and Fargo kept up his informal walking-sentry duty. One by one, lanterns and candles winked out, and the darkness grew thick as new tar. Soon all Fargo could hear was the monotonous crackle of insects and the rise-and-fall hissing of the wind.

All seemed quiet enough, but Fargo had grown even more suspicious after his talk with Childress and McGinnis. Dill Stover could easily get inside with help from "solid citizens" such as those two.

Fargo hadn't considered the possibility of Indian attack, not against walled and well-protected Mormon Station. But just then a coyote yipped, so close it had to be just beyond the wall. *Or is it only a good imitation,* Fargo wondered.

He moved to the nearest gun port in the wall and glanced outside. Spectral moonlight turned Great Salt Lake into a million sparkling diamonds. But Fargo saw no one or nothing that didn't belong to the place. Thus reassured, his thoughts naturally turned to Dora and her ample charms.

It was late enough to look her up, Fargo figured. He angled off the path and hooked around to Dora's window on the south side of the house.

Again the long, yipping bark of a coyote. So close it sounded like it was inside the wall. *Could be Indians signaling to each other,* Fargo reasoned. They sometimes made daring raids and took white prisoners to exchange for Indian captives.

But they almost never attacked a walled settlement. And Dora's window was inviting Fargo.

First, on a gut hunch, he climbed back into his own room and got his Henry rifle. He jacked a round into the chamber. Then he grabbed his rolled-up blanket, returned to the side of the house, and rapped on the pane of Dora's room lightly with his knuckles.

Fargo feared the travel-worn woman might have passed out. But in seconds she was at the moonlit window, wearing only an embroidered chemise. Her dark hair, loose now, spilled over her bare shoulders.

"Did you bust your leg in a badger hole?" she teased him in a low but melodic tone. "You were gone for hours."

"Had to make sure it's safe for us to play, didn't I?" he explained, fully aware of her hyacinth-smelling hair and perfumed skin. Also the way the sheer chemise outlined her protuberant nipples.

"Did I wake Sarah up?" he added as he set his rifle against the house, then reached in and lifted Dora out the window. It was easy as lifting a fistful of feathers.

"Sarah? That kid sleeps through blizzards. My goodness, Skye, you'll make me dizzy, swinging me about so."

Fargo set her down and handed her the blanket, then picked up his rifle and carried it muzzle down as they headed through the grass toward the irrigation ditch behind a screen of cedars. Fargo froze in midstep at yet another series of yipping barks, sounding even closer this time.

"Trouble?" Dora asked nervously, watching him. "Not that I want to go back inside."

"Should be as safe back here as anywhere else," Fargo assured her.

He used his Arkansas Toothpick to soften up the ground under their blanket. But Dora did him one better, slipping off and returning with an armful of new hay. Fargo laid his short gun and Henry within reach, then joined his randy lass in the hay.

"My stars!" she exclaimed when her exploring hand found the hard tent in Fargo's buckskin trousers. "You're already raring to go."

"Been this way since meeting you yesterday," Fargo assured her in a lust-thickened voice. "So if you don't mind, pretty lady, I'm gonna skip the parsley and head right for the main course."

"Do me any darn way you want, you handsome adventurer," she moaned as Fargo slipped the chemise over her head. "Just so you *do* me."

42

She was an alluring little package in the moonlight. That alabaster skin and raven-black hair, the pouty lips and wing-shaped eyes, those large, high-riding breasts on a frame barely five-feet tall. Like many brunettes, Dora had a generous mons bush, forming a mysterious vee that pointed out the magic spot.

Shedding all inhibitions as Fargo's kisses and caresses stoked her loin heat, Dora scissored open her legs to give him a tantalizing view of the glistening folds between them. Her jaw dropped in astonishment when Fargo opened his fly and released his straining manhood.

"I've heard stories about well-endowed men," she whispered, petting it almost reverently, "but I didn't know they grew them *this* big."

"You grew this one, but it'll be smaller soon," Fargo promised her as he fit himself into his favorite saddle and flexed his buttocks, parting her warm, slippery walls and coaxing a keening cry of bliss from her.

Warm, tight, tickling pleasure thrummed in Fargo's groin as he increased his tempo and rhythm, Dora egging him on with her frequent climaxes and the way she locked her ankles behind his back. He slid his hands behind her hard, round little ass and placed one palm under each buttock to lift her higher, lift her even tighter against him as he filled her with probing fire.

"Oh, you're ready, Skye!" she gasped excitedly when she felt his length turn even harder inside her—steel hard. "And it's been a while since you've had release, I can feel it. Here! Let's make it . . . a *big* one! Oh, *ohh*! There, right there! . . ."

She backed up her big talk with sweet action, suddenly using her love muscle to squeeze Fargo's highly charged shaft. Explosions of pleasure drove him to increased exertions, and Dora started firing off climaxes so rapidly she was writhing like a woman possessed.

It had indeed been a longer than usual sexual drought for the Trailsman. There'd been no females in the Humboldt River country, not even Indians. Fargo had begun eyeing a knothole in the latrine door. But he made up for the dry spell now as he spent himself in powerful releases that left him lazy and weak, dreamy and blissful, his mind and all its worries briefly banished.

Eventually, though, Dora's lazy, satisfied voice nudged him back to the present.

"Lord, Skye, you do know how to turn the keys—*all* of them," she teased him. "Is there anything you can't do well?"

"Hell yes. For starters, I can't seem to avoid making enemies," he replied truthfully.

Fargo sat up and studied the night with a practiced eye. A pale sliver of moon and an infinite explosion of stars gave some light, but failed to illuminate the shadowed backlots within the long, serpentine wall. The day-night temperature range was vast in deserts, and Dora—her carnal fires banked for now—was shivering in her chemise. Fargo dropped the blanket over her.

"What's got you worried?" she asked, watching him buckle on his gun belt and leather his Colt after checking the action.

"Experience," he replied honestly. "I'm a lovable, peace-seeking cuss by nature."

"I'll vouch for the lovable part."

"But somehow, I always end up locking horns with stone-hearted killers. Most often in towns."

"Bluenosed biddies and soft-bellied clerks—that's what you'll find in towns, my father used to say," Dora told him. "He called townies 'boardwalkers' and said they'd starve and go naked without stores."

"Mostly your father got it right although I've patronized some of those stores myself."

"Your belly sure hasn't turned soft," she flirted.

A shadow seemed to detach itself from the larger mass of darkness, on the opposite side of the ditch, and glide toward the water. But Fargo decided it was just a tree branch swaying in the wind.

"I looked in my peeping stone while you were gone earlier," Dora said. "Maybe thinking erotic thoughts about handsome men isn't the right mood to get it working. Anyhow, I didn't see a thing about August tenth or anything else."

Only a faint crease in Fargo's forehead revealed he was laughing. Like an Indian at a treaty ceremony, Fargo employed the silent "abdomen laugh" when he was being polite to greenhorns. Secretly, he was almost convinced Dora was making up the chilling "peeping stone" images to eventually make a name for herself—perhaps even a fortune.

Just then the Ovaro whinnied, and Fargo, recognizing the special tone of it, felt his scalp tighten and tingle.

The Ovaro had whiffed bear grease—Indians were almost certainly nearby, probably within the walls.

Fargo catapulted to his feet and crouched with the Henry at the ready, studying his surroundings.

"What?" Dora demanded, alarmed.

"Shush it and stay right there. I—"

The actual attack happened faster than a finger snap, but thanks to the Ovaro's timely warning moments ago Fargo was ready. For just a fractional second he spotted a fierce-looking warrior only about thirty feet away and naked to the waist. Short and heavyset—mountain Ute, almost surely. He wore only leggings, knee-length moccasins, and a breechclout.

Fargo also glimpsed the stone-tipped lance just as the Ute flung it at him.

Fargo twisted himself to one side, the lance tearing a flap off his shirt.

"Stay down!" Fargo barked at Dora, palming out his Colt. The weapon spat orange muzzle streaks as Fargo made it warm for the attacker.

Each time he fired he rolled to a new position. Thus Fargo soon spotted a second Ute, crouched in the high grass about fifteen feet from the first one. Fargo also noticed something else, something curious: both Utes were carrying Colt revolving-cylinder rifles. They could easily have shot him, but they didn't. Obviously, if possible, they wanted to avoid burning powder and alarming the settlement.

That much made sense. But the settlement had been alarmed by now, and lights were starting to show. Raiding Indians, especially just two like this in a well-armed settlement, usually fled at the first sign they'd been discovered.

Yet, these two meant to stand pat. Even now they were desperately looking for him. It puzzled Fargo because it made no sense—unless these weren't chance raiders, but paid assassins with help from within and only one target: Skye Fargo.

Just then they spotted him, peeking out from the tall grass, and opened fire with their rifles.

A hammering racket of gunfire made Fargo's ears ring. Bullets *zwipped* past his ears as he rolled to a new spot, coming up with the Henry this time. The wooden stock slapped his cheek, and spent cartridges peppered the grass all around him, as Fargo rapidly levered and fired.

Once again the high-capacity magazine proved to be the survival edge. Fargo glimpsed both Indians fleeing into the shadows near the wall.

"You okay, Dora?" he called out.

"My God, Skye! I thought the shooting would never stop. Was it Dill Stover?"

"Ute Indians," he replied as he joined her again. "They might still be here, but I doubt it with half the settlement awake by now."

Fargo had no intention of trapping them here. It was never a good idea to corner mountain Utes. The word "surrender" was not part of their vocabulary. Much like the Apaches just south of here, they were famous for their fanatical last stands.

"But what do they want?" Dora asked.

"Damn good question," Fargo admitted. "This trail's taking enough turns to make a cow cross-eyed."

"Wait a minute here," Dora protested. "There's a wall with a manned gate. How could Indians get inside, and back out, without being seen?"

"Yeah, that's a neat trick, innit?"

In truth, none of these recent attacks by Utes made much sense to Fargo. The Utes had gotten along fairly well with this region's newly arrived whites, especially the Mormons. It was the Plains Indians whom Utes hated most.

"I'm nearly naked!" Dora exclaimed. "And here comes a crowd of strict Mormons."

Voices bubbled in the distance, and swinging lanterns approached through the night like drunk fireflies.

"Let's get you back to your room," Fargo said, taking her arm. "The Beckmanns are awake by now, so they'll catch us. But fornication is against Mormon law, they'll lock us both up."

"Skye?"

"Hmm?"

"I just realized—those Indians didn't have to attack you.

They *meant* to. That's why they came here tonight, isn't it? To kill you and you alone?"

"Distinct possibility," Fargo agreed, surprised at her clear grasp of the situation. "But turn over a rock and you'll usually find the slugs clinging beneath. I'd wager these Ute hardcases are doing some white man's bidding."

About four days' travel south of Mormon Station, at the opposite end of the huge lake, dawn was breaking over the vast salt plains surrounding Salt Lake City. A striking redhead, wearing a low-cut dress with velvet-trimmed cuffs, stood in the embrasure of a bay window, watching the rammed-earth streets outside thicken with activity even at this hour.

Lily Snyder could see the big sign in the yard out front, advertising this rambling boardinghouse on Commerce Street. As an outlander she had found it nearly impossible to land a job here. Only her willingness to work for room and board alone had swayed the husband and wife who owned the place.

Even then, at first Lily had despaired of ever finding a way to right the terrible wrong done to her beloved Jimmy. A wrong, she was convinced, that Mormon law would never punish. But she had discovered that grass could push over a stone—it required only time.

And time was all she had left after a monster named Childress took everything from her. A scrawled note found in Jimmy's pocket was all the proof she needed—his last message to the world.

"You, Lilian!"

The words, and harsh tone, cracked like a shot through the downstairs parlor. Lily forced the hate out of her face and turned to confront Esther Emmerick, her horse-faced, middle-aged employer. Usually Esther was merely strict. Lately, however, she was becoming unbearable.

"What?" Lily said wearily, sick of this woman's bullying bluster.

"*What?* How many times have I told you not to dress like a whore in my house? I can see half of your . . . chest. How can my male guests keep their thoughts pure when a harlot is showing them her private parts?"

"Oh, pee doodles," Lily scoffed. "None of the men has complained, not to me."

Esther was laced so tight that her plain black dress rustled when she moved.

"The *men*?" she repeated. "Why would they? You're young and shapely in that sluttish way the devil urges them to admire. Sadly, in the matter of lewd dress, even Mormon women have strayed."

Lily kept the smirk out of her face. That old blowhard Brigham Young had launched tirade after tirade against "frivolous adornment" in dress. But this was one battle the church was losing. The otherwise obedient Mormon women had rebelled on this point—Brigham Young's wives included.

However, Lily knew damn well the real reason why Esther was such a she-witch lately, and in her woman's heart she couldn't blame her. Her husband, Hiram, was now a "wiving Mormon," having just married his second wife. A young and pretty wife who was getting most of Hiram's attention.

"Look at this floor," Esther spat out, "and tell me you have time to gaze dreaming out windows?"

Lily did look. Brass cuspidors were placed everywhere. But judging from the stained floor planks, few men could aim worth a damn.

"The men do no better in the water closets," Lily observed.

"Keep the indecent sarcasm to yourself. I want that floor scrubbed," Esther said, "before the race crowd fills the house this coming weekend."

"Did somebody steal your rattle when you were a baby?" Lily muttered.

"What?"

"I said it'll be done on time."

Lily was sick to death of hearing about their damn horse race. If these Latter-day dry-as-dusts knew how to kick up their heels a little, they wouldn't always be so starved for excitement. The biggest "social event" around here recently was an ax-throwing contest.

Esther thumped toward the kitchen to harass the cook, also an outlander and the primary target of Esther's frustration lately. Her feather duster barely in motion again, Lily returned to her favorite window. Much of the wooden city, a result of Mormon building bees, was visible from here. Just past the Emmerick boardinghouse began the "ladies mile," more like two long blocks than a mile. Already this shopping district buzzed with carryalls and light dearborns. Few late sleepers in Salt Lake City.

By pressing her nose into the glass Lily could also see the spot, between two forks of City Creek, where Brigham Young ordered the temple built. Given her secret activities, it worried Lily that a new symbol for the church was a giant eye—the eye of the "big boss" as she had heard some rebellious Saints call Brigham Young.

Esther's voice screeched behind her. "Lilian! Lazing at that window again?"

"Thought I saw a streak on the glass," Lily fibbed.

"What's the use?" Esther snapped. "I can't strike a spark where there isn't any flint."

"Plenty of flint in you, you old, dried-up—"

"What's that? Speak up, you're always mumbling."

"Nothing," Lily said, dusting in earnest now. "It's just that I'm already soap maker, chandler, parlor maid, serving woman, and in charge of cleaning all the silver. Now you're adding scrubwoman to my duties. When am I supposed to have any *fun?*"

Esther's dark eyes snapped sparks. "*Fun?* My God is the hard God of Moses, young woman."

No need to get your bowels in an uproar, Lily thought crossly. She had a mission to complete, but even so she had suffered from cooped-up fever for months now. Mormons were not all ogres, she reluctantly admitted, especially the nice ones like Saunders Lee. But their ways were strict. The time between sunrise and sunset was for work; nights were for praying, procreating, and sleeping, not socializing.

"What's that?" Esther demanded, pointing at one of Lily's dress pockets.

Lily glanced down and felt her face drain cold when she spotted one edge of a little booklet protruding from the pocket. If she were caught with it, her plan could be ruined and her freedom ended. That was *never* supposed to leave its secret hiding place in Civic Lecture Hall. She'd forgotten to put it back before returning to the house at sunrise.

And if Esther demanded to see it . . . Lily's emerald eyes

shifted to her cleaning basket. Tucked underneath the rags and brushes was a Colt Pocket Model six-shooter. Jimmy gave it to her before he left Illinois for California.

"What is it?" Esther demanded again. "It looks like more of that scandalous 'poetry' by Jack Donne."

"It's just dress patterns," Lily said matter-of-factly.

"More useless frippery to tempt men," Esther barbed. "*Good* morning, Elder West," she added in a changed tone as a tall, sober-suited, gray-bearded man entered the parlor.

He greeted both women, his eyes lingering on Lily's décolletage. Then he shook open his copy of the *Deseret News*, the first newspaper in the Utah Territory.

"Have you read about it, Sister Emmerick?" Elder West said.

His finger pointed to the headline: MIRACLE AT MORMON STATION?

"Skye Fargo is back," he added. "And he'll be coming to Salt Lake City."

"Yes, I saw it. Well, that man is an egregious sinner," Esther said with a sniff. "Put him in the vicinity of a willing woman"—her eyes cut to Dora—"and . . . well, I needn't say. *But*—Skye Fargo put his life on the line for us Saints, down in the border country, and that's more than most gentiles would do for us. He's a welcome guest in this house."

Elder West nodded enthusiastically. "Just so, just so. He's too libertine to practice our creed, but he's been a good friend to Deseret."

Lily, trailing the two of them toward the kitchen, felt a cool feather of alarm tickle her spine. Skye Fargo, coming here? Literally "here," for this was the only boardinghouse allowed to accept gentiles. She knew his reputation for disrupting criminal enterprises. Would he be here in thirteen days, on the anniversary of Jimmy's death?

It won't matter, she decided. She knew how to distract men if need be. And soon—less than two weeks now—her placid, punkin-butter monotony would end decisively.

7

"These damnable grogshops," said Elder Winslowe, "are always remotely located where it's impossible for our marshals and soldiers to sneak up on them. And our soldiers report these swill chutes are protected by at least four men armed so heavily they can fire, virtually without pause, more than one-hundred rounds."

Fargo nodded. "It's profitable, that's why they fight back so hard. An Indian with a hankering to get drunk will trade his best warhorse for a cup of rotgut."

Fargo's lake-blue gaze swept the Great Basin in the metallic glare of morning sunlight. The desert here, east of Great Salt Lake, was not quite so barren as west of the lake. Sometimes the red-sand and white-salt expanses were dotted with thickets of mesquite and clumps of purple sage. For the time being, Fargo rode beside Winslowe, whose practical carryall was pulled by six yoked oxen.

"Well, whoever's selling strong water to the Indians around here," Fargo said, "is also stocking *tiswin*. That's corn beer, an Apache favorite. Since this isn't the Apache home range, why brew it for them?"

"To lure them up here and stir up trouble, that's why," Elder Winslowe replied. Despite the furnace heat, he wore the traditional black broadcloth and white linen. "They're superb desert fighters."

Fargo nodded, letting the Ovaro have his head in this unfamiliar country so he could snuff the ground. A horse settled down quickly once it had the smell of a place.

The Trailsman silently chafed at his inability to safely perform any extended scouting. There was trouble out ahead, he was sure of it. At the first dull, leaden light of dawn they had set out, and a few hours later Fargo began spotting faint dust puffs well ahead.

But he dare not ride out of sight of the others. If some better marksmen were along, Fargo could scout more. Elder Winslowe had courage and an old breech-loading pistol, and John Beckmann, though green as County Cork, would do his best with his mule-ear Kentucky rifle.

But a fourth man, riding a ginger gelding behind the big wagon, wasn't even armed. Orrin Lofley, taciturn, unmarried, in his thirties, was a cooper at Mormon Station. With crowds pouring in from all over the region for the upcoming race this weekend in Salt Lake City, beer would be sold, and plenty of extra barrels were needed.

No, Fargo couldn't risk leaving the group. Women and kids—especially kids—were too great a lure. Four kids would sell high to the Comancheros of nearby New Mexico Territory.

"Skye?" Dora called out from the back of the open conveyance. Thanks to Mormon charity, she and the Beckmann family had new shoes and clothing. "Why are you staring so hard and long out ahead? Yesterday, you were always looking behind."

"I'm looking both ways, lady," he assured her. "But I'm looking out ahead plenty because I think Indians are following us."

Puzzled, Dora laughed. "Following us? Then why look ahead?"

"Even I know that answer," her brother-in-law spoke up, eager to share his copious reading. "Indians sometimes 'follow' a person by guessing where he's going, then riding out ahead. It's safer than being behind because your quarry can't lay in ambush for you to catch up."

Fargo was impressed that John knew such things. Just then his eagle-eyed vision spotted something well out ahead. A minute later his stomach went cold—he had a sinking feeling he knew what it was.

"Don't be in any big hurry to catch up with me," Fargo muttered to Winslowe. Then he kicked the Ovaro up to a trot across the hot, crystalline sand.

His stallion, getting a good whiff of the sage, wanted to run. Fargo let him stretch his muscles for a few minutes. Then he reined in and stared at the unspeakable sight of another lone traveler murdered, his brains beaten out with stones. The genitals had been severed and stuffed into his mouth.

Most likely Utes or maybe Paiutes did it, Fargo thought, studying the desolate terrain encircling them while he fought off a surge of nausea. But it was the images of Dill Stover, Frederic Childress, and Cecil McGinnis that filled the screen of his mind. The likely "prime movers" behind these crimes lately.

Fargo quickly gathered rocks and heaped them over the body so the women and kids wouldn't have to see this horrific mess. Hell, he wished *he* hadn't seen it.

Elder Winslowe's carryall rocked to a stop, his adult passengers staring at the rock mound. Fargo was grateful that all four kids, still tuckered out, were sound asleep on a feather mattress.

"Savages?" the normally silent Orrin Lofley asked from horseback, glancing nervously around.

Fargo nodded. He kept his tone low to avoid waking the kids. "All of us best keep a weather eye out, hear? There's a Ute keeping an eye on us as I speak. And he's most likely taking his orders from a white man."

"Which white man?" Elder Winslowe demanded. "The territorial government will put him on trial."

Fargo was nearly convinced that Frederic Childress was *the* boy behind the regional trouble, with plenty of help from so-called Mormon newspaperman Cecil McGinnis and dirt-worker Dill Stover. And no doubt others. But Childress was also a respected merchant in Deseret, very high status indeed. Fargo would make no accusations until he could back them up.

"I'll have some names for you soon enough, Elder," Fargo promised, eyes scanning sand dunes to the right of the wagon. "Meantime, keep your eyes to all sides. Utes are no boys to mess with."

The four of them met in the arid foothills of the Wasatch Range, secluded in a little gulch lined with piñons: Frederic Childress, Dill Stover, and the renegade mountain Utes known as He Bear and Nothing but Trouble. No one looked happy. After three botched attempts to kill Fargo, the normally placid Childress was growling like a sore-tailed bear.

"For all your bragging, Dill," he flung at Stover, "you sure are poor shakes as a shootist, know that? You missed Fargo in broad daylight. Is this an example of how you mean to shine in the Salt Lake Run?"

"With Fargo, see, it was on accounta them damn crickets—"

"You can pull excuses out of your hip pocket, can't you? Are you getting snow in your boots, Dill, is that it? Afraid of Fargo's 'bigger than life' reputation?"

Stover, looking sullen and put-upon, peeled a twig with his teeth and said nothing. He wore dirty sailcloth trousers and a gray cotton fatigue shirt from his brief stint in the army. One palm rested on the butt of his Smith & Wesson Volcanic—the two Utes, as usual, were making sheep's eyes at his horse and his scope-equipped Big Fifty. They meant to steal both, all right, first chance he gave them.

"Dill, a man's reputation has never stopped a bullet," Childress insisted.

The merchant, coat unbuttoned, sat on the seat of his buckboard. The bed was filled with stolen U.S. military food rations as well as wooden water casks—except that most of the casks were filled with Indian burner going to a pair of grogshops near Weber Canyon.

"Fargo has to be planted," Childress added, "and the sooner the better."

"You ain't just a-woofin', boss," Stover agreed, still watching the Utes like a cat on a rat. "We *can't* quit now. Once Fargo starts working a trail, nobody stops him."

"Yes, I've deduced that by now. Either we finish it or he will."

"Maybe a red-hot running-iron is what he needs," Stover said. "Pressed right into those eyes of his that see too damn much."

"I favor a quick, efficient kill, no fancy stuff to call attention to it. I have several business interests to protect, including five-hundred new rifles that will be seized if I'm caught with them."

Childress, his pale-agate eyes cold and cunning, turned to study the Utes, both of whom spoke some English. They held their ponies by the buffalo-hair hackamores. Both mounts were ugly little broom-tails, dish-faced and ill-tempered. But

Childress knew these "Indian scrubs" were peerless when it came to endurance, even matched against mules.

"You," he said to the largest of the pair, He Bear, "is your cousin watching them right now as you promised?"

He Bear nodded. Like his companion he wore double-soled, knee-length, elkskin moccasins.

"Sioux Killer good spy," he said. "Send mirror signals."

Childress studied both Indians, looking for any signs they were lying.

"Last night, in Mormon Station," he chided, "your noisy failure to kill Fargo left *all* of us holding the crappy end of the stick."

"*You* kill him," Nothing but Trouble challenged.

"Be more like the fierce Apaches," Childress challenged him right back, "not like the cowardly Poncas or these praying Indians in New Mexico. Only the Apaches successfully resisted the long Spanish invasion."

Nothing but Trouble touched his colorful sash, heavy with dangling hair. The custom, once a scalp had been properly cured, was to die the hair a brilliant gold or crimson.

"These two," Nothing but Trouble said, pointing to a pair of gold ones, "were Apaches."

"All right, so you live up to your name, do you? Then prove it by killing Fargo, and do it soon."

The two braves exchanged a long glance. White men are fools, that glance said. They wrap their feet in thick leather hides, so they can neither feel ground vibrations nor move silently. Even when standing right next to each other, they are always shouting. And talk? Whereas a red warrior welcomed silence, white men would say anything just to hear their own voices.

But white men also had liquor, tobacco, guns, sugar, coffee, and so much more. The Utes had first met Childress at his grogshop down south near the Old Spanish Trail. He gave them work on the spot. Life had been much easier since then.

"Yes or no?" Childress demanded.

"Ahh, piss on them ignut blanket asses," Dill Stover piped up. "*I'll* pop Fargo, all right. The hell's the odds of crickets next time?"

"We kill him," He Bear answered for both Utes. As was

55

the custom, he left his thoughts and emotions out of his face. Only women, children, and white men were weak enough to reveal their feelings in their faces.

He Bear added, "But he seem good man, good warrior."

"Don't you believe it," Childress assured him. "Oh, sure, he can kill. But he is among those who see the Indians as dangerous animals to be exterminated. Your people have tried the peace road with them. All you have to show for it are empty bellies and stolen homelands."

"Here you go, John," Stover called over, using the white man's name for all Indian males. "For your *empty* belly."

Unobserved, Stover had pulled a shoulder of salt-cured pork out from the supplies in the buckboard. As he walked toward the Utes, grinning and waving it around, both braves paled and moved quickly away from him.

"Knock it off, Dill," Childress said, though he, too, was grinning. Many Indians were disgusted by pork and its light color. Some believed the army inspection stamp was in fact a tattoo, and that the "pork" meat was actually white man.

"*Mmm . . .* son of a *bitch* that's good fixens," Stover said, gnawing off a hunk and chewing it with his mouth wide open. "Tastes better than Ma ever did."

He Bear turned away and made retching sounds.

"All right, put it away, Dill," Childress snapped. "I want all three of you to head west and start living in constant sight of Fargo's group. And I'll tell you something else: I don't want to see *any* of you again until the world can see Skye Fargo's soles."

After the meeting, Childress pointed his team south toward Weber Canyon. Stover, mistrustful of all Indians on principle, immediately headed east riding by himself.

But the two Utes, needing to discuss some things, lingered behind and let their ponies graze. They both sat in the shaded grass and smoked to the Four Directions, inhaling deeply of sweet kinnikinnick mixed with tobacco. At first they spoke only of trifling matters.

Then He Bear set the pipe on the ground between them, the sign that serious talk could begin.

"Brother," he said in the Ute tongue, "have ears for my words. When did I ever hide in my lodge while my brothers struck the warpath?"

"Never," Nothing but Trouble affirmed. "When you die, your face will be toward your enemies."

"As you say. These dirt-scratchers whites call Mormons are not so bad toward the red man. But these 'Americans' who come from the land beyond the sun's birthplace—most of them I kill like snakes, for they mean to wipe out our kind."

He Bear paused and shrugged one muscular shoulder. Though short, he was powerfully built. "However, this man called Far-go . . . true, I have no zeal for killing him. Yet, I will because the reward will be great. But this thing must be done cautiously."

Nothing but Trouble mulled this for some time. "Straight words, brother. He is a favorite with the dirt-scratchers."

He Bear nodded. "It will go hard on the man who kills him. Stover has made his boast, before others, how he means to kill this hair-face. So we"—he paused to nod toward the Colt rifle lashed to his pony—"will kill like white men. And let all eyes turn toward Stover."

"But even now Stover is on his way. He may kill him first."

"Then let him. But I do not think Stover can best the bearded one. His hair will be *our* trophy."

Neither brave had to say what would happen to the others with Fargo. The men would be killed, the children sold to Comancheros, the women raped and then "slain into silence."

Having said all they needed to, both Utes swung onto their ponies and headed west.

"Is he still out there, Skye?" Dora asked.

Fargo nodded, sleeving sweat off his forehead. "Yep. And I've got a hunch others are out there somewhere, too, including Dill Stover. Evidently I'm the meat that lures the tiger."

The wagon road was bad, often broken by gullies and hampered by thick clumps of sage. As they crossed a big lava bed, Fargo reined in his stallion and swung down to study the hard ground.

"How can you find prints here, Skye?" Dora asked. "It's like stone."

"I can't, not full prints. But besides prints you'll find nicks, scratches, turned-over pebbles, discolorations where

57

horses or men make water. Everyone leaves a trail of some kind, even across stone."

Orrin Lofley spurred his ginger forward from the drag position.

"I think someone was riding behind us for awhile," he reported. "He's gone now."

Fargo nodded, gazing all around them in the dry, brittle heat. "Yeah, I spotted reflections back there. Just like the kind silver saddle trim gives off. Take care back there, Orrin. I recommend that you avoid riding in a straight line for too long."

"Silver trim?" Estelline repeated. "Dill Stover?"

Fargo swung up into leather again. "Yep. Dill Stover, I'd lay odds."

"I don't trust that man," Elder Winslowe remarked. "And *not* because he's an outlander. He'll be coming to Salt Lake City for this weekend's race," Winslowe added. "In fact, he's an early favorite. Or rather, his superb horse is. Nobody around here cares much for the man."

The race . . . Fargo had decided this was as good a time as any to face the inevitable. Much of his ready cash had gone to purchase woefully overpriced emergency rations from Childress three days ago. And now that he was on another foolish "mercy mission" to get these folks safely settled, he'd need paying work of a temporary nature. And this race, with its impressive two hundred and fifty dollar purse, fit the bill nicely.

It might also put him in a showdown with Stover, and Fargo welcomed the chance.

"No offense to your people, Elder Winslowe," Dora remarked, glancing around them with a despairing face. "But I just can't see why *anyone* would ever settle out here. Or even be interested in exploring it."

"You're looking at one reason," Fargo told her, nodding toward the sunlit expanse of Salt Lake. "The first explorers into this region were convinced there had to be a waterway between Salt Lake and the Pacific. Would've been a trade-route bonanza."

"Dora's apprehensive mood," Elder Winslowe suggested, a kindly smile peeking through his wild gray beard, "is partly caused by nervousness about how she'll be treated in Salt Lake City. It's true, dear, that Brigham Young is involved in everything down there, which gives him great power over his followers. And *some* of our elders and bishops will do anything to keep the church wealthy and powerful. But you'll discover that the rank and file are mostly good people."

Elder Winslowe excused himself, swung down from the carryall, and walked out behind a sand dune to relieve himself.

"He seems a nice enough gent," Dora told Skye. "But *how* can he call them good people when they do something so . . . pagan and primitive as practice polygamy? *How* could civilized people even consider it?"

"Survival," John chimed in. "The point is to increase the number of Mormons so they dominate politically."

Fargo grinned. "No big surprise that men are for it, huh? But so many Mormon women, too, prefer the arrangement. Something's crossways there. Anyhow, most of the stories back east are exaggerated. I'm told, by honest Mormons, that only about two men out of a hundred can afford to be wiving Mormons."

While they waited for the elder to return, Fargo took a careful squint all around them. He saw nothing alarming, yet he was convinced the stinking sage rats were out there, all right. And now there were low, mesquite-covered hills on their left flank—perfect for ambush.

Orrin was an especially vulnerable target. Fargo knew how hard it was to distinguish features in this shimmering heat and glare—an isolated horsebacker might be mistaken for him. He wheeled the Ovaro and headed back toward Lofley.

"Seen anything, Orrin?"

"A few reflections," the cooper replied.

At first Fargo had wondered about Lofley—what kind of soft-brained fool went unarmed in the dangerous American West? But so far the quiet man had remained calm and steady, showing little fear. And he was excellent with horses—even the people-wary Ovaro took an instant shine to Orrin. Fargo was beginning to like the man although he sure wished Lofley was heeled—every gun helped.

"I'd feel a mite easier," Fargo said, "if you'd ride up

closer to the rest of us. Isolated the way you are, it'd be too easy to drop a bead on you. I don't want you or anyone else taking a bullet meant for me."

"Skye!" John Beckmann bellowed from up ahead. "Great jumping Judas, *look*!"

The teacher pointed toward the mesquite hills east of them. About five or six hundred yards across the hard-baked wasteland, a Ute Indian sat his pony.

"Wouldja look at that red son," Fargo remarked, a tinge of admiration in his tone. "Showing himself in bullet range, bold as a big man's ass."

The Indian reined his pony around and began heading back into the hills at a leisurely pace. He wasn't close enough for Fargo to see if he was one of the Utes who tried to kill him last night at Mormon Station.

"Going after him?" Orrin asked.

Fargo shook his head. "I ain't taking the oat bag. He's a lure. When I ride close enough, another Ute will rise up out of a rifle pit and put at me. Best not to fight an Indian on his terms—you'll generally lose. Besides, I got no proof that's even a hostile. He's showing no weapons."

Orrin opened his mouth to reply. An eyeblink later, his face disappeared in a red smear! Right behind the bullet came the whip-crack of a high-caliber rifle.

"Jesus!" a shocked Fargo exclaimed even as gouts of hot, sticky blood sprayed his face.

One of the women screamed, and Orrin immediately folded out of the saddle, landing in an awkward heap on the desert floor.

"Cover down!" Fargo shouted to the rest. "Keep the kids under you!"

A quick glance verified that it wasn't the Ute doing the shooting—he, too, had turned around to look, surprise starched into his features. Fargo calmed the spooked ginger, then swung down to look at Orrin.

He assumed the Mormon must be dead, but incredibly, he was still barely breathing. A pink, bloody froth bubbled on his lips, and Fargo knew the lung air was mixing with blood—Orrin was doomed.

He was still kneeling over the fallen man when Fargo's low-crowned hat flew off his head, followed by the crack of a second shot. A hot line across his scalp marked where the bullet had grazed him.

"About thirty seconds between shots," Fargo muttered. "The same time it takes to reload and aim a Sharps Big Fifty."

Fargo yanked his brass-framed army field glasses out of a saddle pocket and studied the distant mesquite hills until he detected a blue streamer of smoke. Then he tugged the Henry from its saddle boot, levered a round into the chamber, and took up a prone position to lower his profile.

Over and over the Henry kicked into his shoulder as Fargo peppered the position. He had no chance of hitting anyone, nor could his 200-grain powder loads be counted on to kill at this range. But few snipers could relax and shoot well with lead whistling in around them.

Faint dust puffs told him the shooter—almost surely Dill Stover—had just ridden off, chased away by Fargo's volley. Cautiously, seeing Fargo stand up again, Elder Winslowe, John, and Dora climbed out of the conveyance, Estelline staying with the children.

The three joined Fargo just in time to hear the long, awful, rattling sound of Orrin Lofley's last breath as he gave up the ghost.

Winslowe, his voice shaken, said, "*Why* kill Orrin? He's just a barrel maker."

Fargo booted his Henry, weather-bronzed face grim with controlled anger.

"That bullet wasn't meant for Orrin," Fargo said. "The exact color of a horse washes out over distance in this desert glare. Orrin's got a beard something like mine, a dark hat, and we're both about the same size. He was in the wrong place at the wrong time."

"Hell-inspired, cold-blooded *murder*," Elder Winslowe steamed. "Like so many that go unpunished in the West. We'll take him to Salt Lake City for a proper funeral."

Fargo began leading the ginger forward to tie it to the tailgate of the carryall.

"It was cold-blooded murder, all right," he said in a flat tone. "But Orrin Lofley took a bullet for me. And I guaran-damntee it, Elder—his killer *will* be punished. Not under territorial law, either. It'll be gun law."

8

A man's startled curse, then the shattering explosion of John Beckmann's old mule-ear rifle, brought Fargo bounding out of his bedroll, Colt cocked and at the ready.

It was pitch dark, and not too long after Fargo had finished his midnight-to-three A.M. stint of guard duty. He forced the cobwebs of sleep from his mind and tried to read the situation.

"John!" he shouted. "You all right?"

"I—I think so," came his voice out of the desert's nighttime coolness.

"Indians?" Fargo pressed, eyes scanning their camp in a brushy hollow just off the wagon road.

"Looked like it, Skye. Two of them, on foot. I—I didn't shoot *at* them because I wasn't sure. So I fired over their heads and they took off quicker than scat."

Fargo did a quick head count to make sure everyone was still present.

"Whoever it was," Beckmann said as he joined Fargo, "we have your horse to thank. That stallion is some pumpkins as a sentry, Skye. Not only whinnied to warn me, but even pointed his head right at them for me like a hunting dog."

"He alerts to the smell of bear grease," Fargo explained. "I hope Indians don't switch to using something else in their hair."

Estelline began to hustle the yawning kids back into their beds in the carryall. Fargo left Elder Winslowe and John, both of whom were armed, to protect the camp while he moved out onto the surrounding desert plains looking for sign.

The moonlight was stingy tonight, the shadows deep and menacing. But Fargo's experienced eyes soon noticed small, circular depressions in the salt dust, two sets of them—the Utes had walked on their heels to minimize ground noise and obscure their prints. An ambush still wasn't out of the question, so Fargo leapfrogged from creosote bush to piñon clump, his Colt always to hand.

Then he found the spot where they'd ground-hitched their ponies, and saw how their trail led east into the mountains.

"They'll be back," Fargo told the adults when he returned to camp. "They've changed their tactics. Before, they were content to plink at us from a distance. But now we're closer to Salt Lake City, and they're getting worried we might make it. So they tried to catch us in our sleep."

With sunrise Fargo's group would begin their fourth day on the road to Salt Lake City. These past two days, he had quashed the sniping at his companions by riding roving flank guard to either side as the terrain dictated. He himself was shot at twice, one bullet nicking his saddle fender. But Fargo resisted pursuit, wanting to keep his charges in full view as much as possible.

"Skye?"

The unexpected voice of ten-year-old Katy surprised everyone. She must have been listening to them, Fargo realized. He could see the pale oval of her face peeking out of the wagon bed.

"You still awake, button?" Fargo called over.

"Skye, will the Indians get us?"

Estelline stifled a sob. Even Fargo felt a little quivering heat behind his eyes.

"Ah, they're trying, hon," he answered calmly. "But they didn't get past your papa tonight, did they?"

"Nope!" Katy said proudly as she lay down again. "Pa scared 'em away."

"They didn't get past your horse, you mean," John muttered. "I'd never have seen them in time without his warning."

"He's saved me the same way," Fargo reminded him. "You did your job the best you could, and tonight your best was good enough. We're all alive thanks to your vigilance, schoolteacher. Hell, I was dead to the world."

63

He looked around at the others in the silvery moonlight: Elder Winslowe, John, Estelline, Dora—who still wore only her chemise, as if to torment Fargo. It had been impossible for them to renew their erotic acrobatics on the trail. But thoughts of their lovemaking had both of them sizzling for more.

"We should make Salt Lake City by tonight," he told them. "Today will be their last chance to stop us. We'll all need to be alert and hold our trail discipline."

"Will you be staying in Salt Lake, too, Skye?" Dora asked.

For a moment Fargo saw an image of Orrin's face disappearing behind blood. Then the images of all those swollen-tongued and mutilated bodies lying in the burning white sand.

"A little while, yeah," he replied. "First I'll see you folks settled. Then there's some questions I plan to get answered."

Fargo studied the surrounding darkness. "Right now, though, the rest of you folks should turn in. There's still a couple hours till dawn, and you'll need your rest. I'll stand watch."

Fargo kept up a walking patrol while the others slept, fully aware that Indians sometimes attacked the same place again after a failed attempt. Before long he noticed a soft glow in the east like foxfire, the glow called false dawn. It meant the real thing was near. He waited until there was enough light to see his hand in front of his face, then woke the others.

Starting with Dora. She awoke instantly at his touch, taking his hand and guiding it under her chemise to the soft, smooth, exciting swell of her breasts.

"They miss you, Skye," she whispered. "First chance we get, right?"

"Or a little sooner," he promised, reluctantly moving on to wake the others.

By the time hot coffee was brewed and bacon fried, there was enough light to reveal the gruesome sight of Orrin Lofley's body, which Elder Winslowe and John had just finished draping over the ginger gelding. It was wrapped in his mackinaw, with salt dirt packed in as a preservative. Fargo had hated his decision to haul Lofley that way, but it was better than making the kids ride with him in the carryall.

"Try not to harden your heart, Skye," advised Elder Winslowe, seeing Fargo stare at the body as they broke camp. "Most of the Utes are not so violent and bloody."

"It's not them I'm thinking of. Those two braves last night are most likely the same ones who tried to kill me up at Mormon Station. But they're just the hired help."

Elder Winslowe look troubled. "You've mentioned that twice now. You believe it's Frederic Childress stirring all this up, don't you?"

Fargo untethered the Ovaro and watched him do some serious bucking to shake out the night kinks.

"Yeah, I'd wager he's the one with his hands on the reins," Fargo replied. "Why, you think otherwise?"

"Well . . . he's a gentile, of course, and it's easy for *me* to be suspicious that he's breaking our laws. And he goes out into the deserts so often, usually with disreputable men like Dill Stover at his side. But I know of no solid proof against him."

"Let me fill it in," Fargo suggested when Winslowe started to add something, then fell silent. "Since there's a whopping ten percent 'profit tax' on commerce in Deseret, and Childress makes money by the wagon load, he's a favorite with the High Council in Salt Lake City?"

"Even dines occasionally with Brigham Young," Winslowe admitted.

"So he'll have to be caught red-handed," Fargo said. "And in open country like this, that's a rough piece of work. Especially since Childress is slicker than snot on a saddle horn. But slick or not, he'll foul his nest. They always do."

Fargo mounted and led the others up out of the hollow. They were south of the Mormon Trail now, moving away from Great Salt Lake and southeast toward the city. The eroded plateau country lay out ahead of them, vast, haze-shrouded, pocked with ancient canyons white men had yet to lay eyes on.

"Look, Skye!"

Little six-year-old Sarah pointed excitedly from the wagon. "There's white feathers hanging from those bushes! Pretty! Who did it, Skye?"

All eyes were on him, waiting for an answer. But after the three tense days they'd all just spent, and with at least one more day ahead, Fargo hadn't the heart to tell the truth: those "pretty" feathers were tokens, tied there last night by the Utes, to propitiate their gods. And to help assure a victory over this camp.

"They're just Indian decorations, hon," Fargo replied.

But already his lake-blue eyes were in constant motion, watching for the ever-expected attack.

At the same time Skye Fargo had been watching the dawn sky, Lily Snyder was putting the finishing touches on her long-awaited revenge.

Nothing in Salt Lake City, except banks and the armory, was locked up at night. For weeks now Lily had been sneaking into the huge Civic Lecture Hall, where many locals came for a morning bracer of stern moral instruction before the workday began. It hadn't taken her long to discover a large crawl space between the building's high ceiling and the floor of the attic.

And, by now, she was almost ready. Just in time for the first anniversary, in only ten more days, of Jimmy's death.

"No, his murder," she whispered, correcting herself. "A slow, agonizing death from thirst while his tormentor watched. And I have it in Jimmy's own words."

Crouched over in the crawl space between floor and ceiling, Lily looked at her handiwork in the flickering candlelight: a hundred simple, handleless cups she'd made of paraffin. She already had the bright red paint, a big pail of it swiped from a shed—more than enough to fill the paraffin cups. For the Mormons she had nothing lethal planned. Just a symbolic "blooding" for the almost all-male crowd that would be listening on August tenth—a reminder that they, too, had blood on their hands because they allowed monsters like Frederic Childress such a free hand.

As for Childress himself . . . by a fine twist of fate, he was the invited speaker on August tenth. And there would be no red paint for him, just real blood. His own.

She glanced at the trap door above her. All she needed to do was throw a bolt lock open. That would release a ceiling panel that she had laboriously cut out, then put back in place with hinges. The hundred small cups would be stuck to the panel and drop their harmless, but shocking, contents thirty feet onto the crowd below. She, meantime, would be concentrating on Childress, making sure one of her six bullets killed him. He could take his fifteen-dollar cups of water to hell with him, the vicious bastard!

Ten days from today . . .

Despite her determination, fears and doubts plagued her. Mormons made no distinctions in law—women were executed for murder, too.

"To horse!"

The sudden command, from the military barracks and parade ground across the street, did not startle her. Lately, Captain Saunders Lee drilled his men every morning at sunrise. Word of this weekend's race had spread far, and even many outlanders were being lured to Salt Lake City. Brigham Young himself was in the spirit, promising to send up a hot-air balloon for entertainment. The Mormon Battalion would be the main police force.

She hurried up a ladder into the attic and glanced out a small, fan-shaped window. From here she had a good view of City Creek with its gristmills, sawmills, and water-powered threshing machine.

The call "To horse!" had put each man at the head of his mount.

"Prepare to mount!" Lee shouted, and each man fitted a boot to a stirrup and grabbed the horn.

"Mount!"

Lily watched Saunders Lee with grudging admiration as he vaulted neatly onto his cavalry charger. She had to admit he was handsome, honorable, and kind to all, Mormon and gentile alike.

But despite Saunders's many kindnesses toward her, Lily knew her fate if she was caught up here even planning this. She'd be imprisoned for a long time, especially when they found her gun. Even having that lecture schedule, which Esther had spotted in her pocket, would have raised suspicions if Elder West hadn't walked in and distracted Esther in the nick of time.

As if to underscore the point, several prisoners in double irons were led from the stockade to the mess hall.

"Advance by columns of four!" Saunders shouted, and the mounted formation clattered out into the dusty street, faces ghostly gray in the new morning light.

The soldiers are gone for now, she realized, relaxing a bit. But as Lily prepared to return to Emmerick's boarding-house to begin her long work shift, something else began to trouble her.

This Skye Fargo, the Trailsman . . . the newspapers were still abuzz about his coming. The articles claimed that Saunders Lee, before becoming a Mormon, had served in the U.S. Cavalry fighting Sioux, that he and Fargo were friends from those days. Then Saunders was court-martialed for refusing an extermination order and accepting surrenders instead.

Fine, but she didn't like the idea of those two smart, capable men teaming up—not when she had plans to hide. But *let* Fargo come. Likely, her path wouldn't cross his anyway. Besides, from all accounts Fargo was a ladies' man, unlike the duty-obsessed Saunders, and she could distract *that* type, all right. Most men's brains were between their legs.

"Not one damn thing is going to stop me," Lily vowed as she slipped silently out into the ghostly blue street. "Certainly no mere man."

"God dawg, Innuns!" Dill Stover exclaimed as he rode upon their small camp just past daybreak. "The day's still a pup! How's come you're sittin' on your lazy red asses like it's sundown?"

The shorter of the two Utes, Nothing but Trouble, was hardening arrow points in the fire. He looked up, but said nothing.

" 'S'matter, John?" Stover demanded, still sitting his horse. "A rifle's too much for you to handle?"

"As you handled yours yesterday?" He Bear fired back. "When you killed the wrong man? After letting Nothing but Trouble risk his life in the open? You took our shot."

Dill had stolen a couple of bottles of liquor from Childress during the meeting near the Wasatch. Lately he'd been slugging back shots of fiery mash as if it were lemonade—that's what had pulled his aim *just* to the left yesterday.

"So what?" he retorted. "You blanket asses would've botched the shot, anyhow. Just like you botched your little 'raid' this morning."

The braves said nothing. Nothing but Trouble continued turning an arrow point in the tiny fire while He Bear began working a whetstone in smooth swipes along the blade of his knife.

Stover scowled at their apparent apathy. By now he didn't care *who* killed Fargo so long as the dogged son of a bitch went under.

"It's no feather-bed job killing a jasper like Fargo," he warned them. "You won't get it done squatting on your heels."

"Or with big talk," He Bear said pointedly. "Keep your useless words in your sash. Are we young girls in our sewing lodge, discussing the various causes of the wind?"

"You made boasts about killing him," Nothing but Trouble put in. "Now let your rifle speak for your mouth."

Once again, Stover noticed, the renegades were aiming covetous glances at his roan and his scoped Big Fifty. He backed the well-trained gelding up, right hand palming the butt of his Smith & Wesson.

"Goddamn vultures," he said, face twisted with contempt.

He Bear nodded toward Stover's silver-trimmed saddle.

"Vultures? I was there, down on the Green River," he said, "when you shot a Mexican in the back for that saddle, yellow eyes."

The first white men He Bear's tribe ever saw were severely jaundiced mountain men—"yellow eyes."

"A squaw man like you," He Bear added, "is not fit to lick Fargo's boot like a dog. He will kill you, and after we Utes have pissed on your bones, we will kill Fargo."

Stover was too astounded to get angry. Not with two of them to pull against.

"Know what?" he told both Indians. "The Mormons are mealymouthed peckerwoods when it comes to you red Arabs. *Souls?* You sons a bitches need killing, is all. After I put the quietus on Fargo, you two best start chanting your death song."

*   *   *

Fargo knew his would-be killers were getting more desperate as his party rolled ever nearer to Salt Lake City. So he intensified his vigilance as the day wore on.

Elder Winslowe and John Beckmann kept their weapons to hand. They remained especially vigilant each time Fargo rode out on a brief scout, heading off trouble. He found fresh signs that they were being watched, including a small cave oven dug in the side of a hill, still warm.

Once Fargo even spotted game, the first he'd seen in days—a distant herd of antelope, their white-spotted rumps flashing in the sunlight. But, so far today, no actual sighting of the killers.

"They seem to be holding their powder," Fargo remarked to Elder Winslowe and John on his latest trip back to join the others. "Maybe they've given up on daylight attacks."

Winslowe leaped out and guided his team off the road to make way for a stagecoach rocking on its braces—the first they'd seen since leaving Mormon Station. Earlier they had passed a little stage-stop hellhole, in the desert, where a plate of beef, beans, and vegetables sold for five dollars. Fargo's party bypassed it, content to gnaw on the jerked beef, hardtack, dried fruit, and bacon Winslowe packed along.

"Skye?"

Fargo, busy studying the good ambush points surrounding them, glanced at Dora. She rode in the bed of the open carryall where she'd been tending to Estelline.

Fargo kneed the Ovaro around and went back to her. Once again she wore her shiny black hair in two long braids in front of her shoulders. The lively green eyes, however, looked troubled now.

"Estelline's poorly," she almost whispered. Her sister was napping fitfully.

"Is it serious, you think?" Fargo asked.

"I'm not sure. She's had pains since last night. John's scared she might lose the baby."

"Damn," Fargo said, feeling helpless on this one. Of course the poor woman was in danger of miscarrying. The fear for herself and her family, the shock of barbarous sights, the cruel demands of starvation and exhaustion.

"It means we won't get into Salt Lake until tomorrow morning," Fargo decided, looking down at Estelline, "but we're going to take a longer break than usual now so she can rest in some shade without all the shaking. That should have us right near the city outskirts when we camp tonight."

However, before they reached a suitable shady spot, John shouted from out ahead, "Could be trouble, Skye! Somebody lying in the road—he looks dead!"

Fargo, who was just riding off to scout the right flank, loped the Ovaro back down to the wagon road to investigate. The man in question was a young Mohave Indian from the deserts of southeast California.

He wasn't dead, just dead drunk. His pony was hobbled nearby and dying of thirst. It worried Fargo immediately. Quite simply stated, there was no reason for Mohaves to be in this region except for the liquor. If those grogshops weren't closed down, and soon, Fargo knew there *would* be a bloody war in Deseret. And that was probably exactly the point.

Fargo watered the pony and gave the Mohave a few swallows before soaking his head and dragging him well back off the road.

"Is he one of those who attacked us?" Dora asked as the carryall lumbered alongside his position.

Fargo shook his head. "Those are Utes after us. This one's from California."

"Thanks to white man's distilling, not too impressive a 'noble savage' at the moment," Elder Winslowe opined as he watched the young brave with sympathy.

Fargo had to agree. His own long-standing admiration for the free-roaming life of the Indians was tempered by sadness that, before long, it would come to an end. Fighting ability wasn't the issue—hell, the Plains Indian, man for man, was the best warrior in America.

"Their big mistake," John said, "is in failing to grasp the true numbers of the whites. I've read that many tribes out here think whites are simply another tribe to be whipped in a few battles. They're doomed."

Fargo nodded, glancing warily around them. "Just remember, they ain't all doomed yet. Keep your nose to the wind, all of you."

"Is Dill Stover out there, too?" Dora asked.

"Distinct possibility," Fargo said.

They found a shady niche in a sandstone formation and rested for two hours, the men taking turns on sentry duty. At one point Fargo noticed Dora discreetly gazing into her "peeping stone."

"Seen anything else in that pretty gewgaw?" Fargo teased her. " 'Sides your own fetching green eyes?"

"No pretty gals soaked in blood, thank the lord. The pictures have stopped coming ever since we saw the redhead and the calendar."

"Since *you* saw her," Fargo corrected.

She slapped his arm. They sat in shade with their backs to a sandstone pillar.

"Anyhow," she said, "it's down to ten days now until August tenth, the date I saw on the calendar inside my peeping stone."

"So?" Fargo said, not feeling quite as devil-may-care as he acted.

"So something awful is going to happen, and probably in Salt Lake City."

Fargo climbed to his feet, slapping alkali dust off his buckskins.

"Something 'awful' is generally happening most places," he said. "C'mon, folks, let's make tracks!"

Estelline seemed noticeably improved by the delay. For the rest of that long, hot, glaring afternoon, Fargo led his bewildered pioneers past the last sight of Great Salt Lake. Salt Lake City lay straight ahead of them now.

"No more attacks today," Fargo told the rest when they stopped to make their final camp within sight of the city. "That means they'll hit tonight, out here, where the Mormon soldiers can't get 'em in time. So it's two men on guard at all times."

Fargo glanced at Dora. "Stover only wants to kill me. But the Utes are dead set on stealing you, Estelline, and the kids. They'll be rich if they sell you six to the Comancheros. Tonight is their last chance in open desert, so *all* of us better sleep light."

9

Despite Fargo's expectations, an attack did not come that night.

Generous moonlight, a silver peppering of bright stars, and a doubling of the sentries made surprise attack difficult in their wide-open location. But Fargo knew that determined foes were out there somewhere, probably Dill Stover and the two Utes, working separately and biding their time.

Finally, a bloodred sun glimmered into being on the eastern horizon.

"We made it, Skye!" exalted John Beckmann, who had split the last shift of guard duty with Fargo. "And Salt Lake City is literally within sight of us now. They've missed their big chance."

"Let's not spend it till it's ours," Fargo cautioned, even as Dora began waking up Estelline and the kids.

The smile bled from John's face and he lowered his voice. "Trouble?"

"I'd expect it, yeah. This was a good spot, far as preventing any sneak assaults on our camp during the night. But being on the wide-open salt flats also makes us vulnerable to rifle fire from those mesas to our north. And with Utes in the mix, no telling when a strike might come. They love to keep their enemies confused."

"Oh, listen to Gloomy Gus," Dora teased him as she combed out her long, dark hair. "Always counting on trouble."

"It seldom disappoints me," Fargo agreed with a good-morning grin.

He waited until Elder Winslowe was dressed and armed. Then, leaving the other two men to guard the camp, Fargo retrieved the binoculars from his saddlebag. He walked out onto the open desert and made a thorough search in the gathering light.

Dill Stover had slept in position on top of the mesa all night, waiting for this one shot.

And now there was Fargo, a tiny little stick man, from here, who seemed to have been spit right out of the flaming ball of a new sun.

It was a difficult shot in this light, over fifteen-hundred feet, and Stover had already made a bipod of crossed sticks to steady the Big Fifty's muzzle. He rolled the breechblock open and thumbed in a round.

His hands trembled slightly, and the sight embarrassed and angered him. But Stover was fully aware that Fargo, nobody's fool, had to know who was trying to kill him. And each attempt that failed only made it even more crucial to kill the Trailsman before he exacted bloody revenge.

Again, that scene from Mary's Station played in Stover's mind. How he had been hurling insults at Fargo, how he flung a drink at him, and then how everything just turned into a whirlwind as Fargo knocked him sick and silly. When he finally came to, his head throbbing like a Pawnee war drum, somebody had put a dress on him. Some of the men took to calling him Mary's Little Lamb after that. *Bastard, Fargo.*

His hands were steady now. Stover spread himself flat in the white sand and slowly began taking up the trigger slack as he laid his crosshairs on Fargo's chest.

Fargo's binocular search of the surrounding desert turned up nothing suspicious. Then again, he reminded himself, Utes were just like Apaches when it came to moving unseen across "open" country. They specialized in finding the lowest seams and in disguising themselves as natural growth.

There was more light now and Fargo wanted to get this done before he was an easy target to anyone on the mesas. He trained his glasses toward the south, where Salt Lake City sat in a bowllike depression. Commerce barely rested in that town, and even now a few conveyances were rolling along the wide main street. Each night, wolf packs entered the city to hunt, and Fargo could see a boy gathering up the heaps of poisoned meat set out for them.

He turned to head back into camp, feeling uneasy even without proof of trouble. In the corner of his left eye, he thought he caught a brief glimmer of light from the mesas to the north. Not the blinding white glare of silver reflecting—the softer flash of early sun on glass.

Fargo dove for the ground even as he felt a sharp tug at the back of his buckskin shirt, followed by the decisive crack of a powerful rifle.

"God *damn* that slippery bastard!" raged Stover, rolling rapidly onto his side to eject the spent cartridge and thumb home a fresh one.

To hell with Fargo, Stover decided in a burst of frustration. That bastard made it too tough on a distance shooter. But that damned prideful stallion of his, so much like its master—*there* was plenty of target, mister, and a man didn't have to get into rock-throwing distance, neither. Besides, with that pinto dead, Dill wouldn't have to worry about losing the Salt Lake Run this weekend.

He shifted his muzzle toward the Ovaro.

"This one kisses the mistress," Stover vowed as he centered the crosshairs on the stallion's exposed flank.

Fargo wasted no time once he realized Dill Stover (few other men in this region could shoot that accurately) had barely missed him. Unfortunately, those big 700-grain slugs packed the distance, all right, and he might well range one in for score. At least, the Big Fifty required a half minute or so between shots to reload and reaim.

."Cover down!" Fargo shouted to the rest. "Put something between you and those mesas!"

The Ovaro was tethered near the late Orrin Lofley's ginger. Fargo, realizing his stallion's vulnerability, raced in that direction.

Just as he did, he recognized behind him a fast, furious series of *thwack* sounds, and a chill was laid over Fargo's spine. He spun around and watched a flurry of arrows rain in on the conveyance and the camp. Fargo was still a good hundred yards away. Obviously the Utes were attacking, but where the hell were they?

"Make every shot score!" Fargo shouted to John and Elder Winslowe, for neither man had a repeating arm.

But the next shot came from up on the mesa again, kicking up a plume of white dust between the two horses. If the Ovaro hadn't already begun crow-hopping at the Indian attack, the shot would have killed him.

And the next one will, Fargo thought.

"Skye!" Dora screamed, and Fargo glanced toward camp just in time to see Elder Winslowe go down with blood spuming from an arrow to the thigh.

"Oh, Christ!" John exclaimed, his voice pitched high with fright. "There goes the death song—they're going to charge!"

Beckmann was lacking in experience, but his reading knowledge was sound—now Fargo spotted both Utes, stripped naked except for clumps of saltbrush tied to their limbs and heads. John's Kentucky mule-ear exploded, the shell kicking dust into the attackers' eyes. Fargo followed up instantly with a volley of lead from the Henry, snapping the back of the charge. Switching to revolving-cylinder rifles to cover their escape, the two Utes retreated.

"Good shooting, Skye!" John shouted. "I think you winged one of them!"

"Let's count our coups later," Fargo snapped. "Reload and get ready for another attack."

It had now been almost thirty seconds since Dill Stover's first shot at the Ovaro. Fargo realized he could never reach the tethered stallion in time. Nor did he have any bead at all on Stover.

Hardly breaking stride, Fargo snatched the Arkansas Toothpick out of his boot, flipped it hard toward the tethering rein, and had the infinite satisfaction of watching it snap. The bullet-savvy Ovaro needed no commands—he immediately began racing away from the gunfire, avoiding a straight line.

Fargo had a smoke curl in sight now, up on the mesa, and emptied the Henry's magazine in that vicinity. That, and the routing of the Utes, must have convinced Stover to rabbit—no more shots rang out from above.

"That was Stover trying to kill you again, wasn't it?" Dora asked Fargo.

They'd just broken off the arrow and pushed it through Winslowe's thigh. The Mormon Elder bore it stoically, even when Fargo poured the last of his whiskey into the wound.

"Can't prove it yet, but it was Stover, all right," Fargo affirmed. "It's all shaking out pretty clear. The Utes *and* Stover all do the dirty work for Childress. That would explain why all of them are trying to kill me. Plus Stover's got a personal grudge. But the Utes, being Indians, measure corn by their own bushel. They want you women and kids most of all."

"Speaking of the Utes," John said, "aren't we going to chase them? They're on foot in open country."

Fargo shook his head. "I rarely pursue an Indian. They figure white men chasing them must mean to hang 'em. Since most Indians fear nothing more than death by hanging, they turn fanatical to avoid it."

"Look!" John called, pointing south toward Salt Lake City. "A big dust cloud. Riders are headed our way."

Fargo raised his binoculars, focused, then felt a grin tugging at his lips. A detail of about a dozen riders, wearing the butternut dye of the Mormon Battalion, was galloping toward them. And the blond-haired officer leading them was his old friend from the Platte River country, Captain Saunders Lee, Mormon convert. Sound carried well in the desert, and Fargo realized they must have heard the gun battle earlier.

"Soldiers," he told the others. "We might as well wait for them, let Elder Winslowe rest that leg until it clots. The Mormons always bring a physician out with them on these rescue missions."

"Oh!"

Fargo glanced at Dora, wondering why she'd exclaimed. Her face was pale as she dropped her "peeping stone" back into the pocket of her dress.

"Sorry," she muttered. "It's just, it gave me the fantods for a second."

"What did?" Fargo asked.

"I just glanced inside, and there was the girl again—the pretty redhead, drenched in blood."

"Un-hunh. I'm gonna catch my horse," Fargo said, turning his back on her.

"She's real, Skye Fargo!" Dora shouted behind him. "And on August tenth, just nine days from today, something terrible happens to her!"

The soldiers arrived in a boiling cloud of dust, their old Hall breechloaders at the ready.

" 'Preciate it all to hell, boys," Fargo greeted them dryly as they rode up. "Nice to know there's a burying detail in Salt Lake City."

"I knew it had to be you behind all that gunfire, Skye Fargo," a grinning Captain Lee greeted his old friend, swinging down to give him a hearty grip.

"I'm surprised your superiors let you come out here, Saunders," Fargo roweled him. "I thought the High Council didn't want you influenced by my heathen ways?"

"That was before you saved the border settlements from starvation, remember? Now it's said you just saved the grain crop in Salt Lake Valley. Personally, I figure that's malarkey. But at the moment, Skye, Deseret's big hero is a womanizing gentile named Fargo."

The Mormon officer glanced quickly around. "Anyone killed or hurt?"

"Elder Winslowe is in the carryall, took an arrow to the thigh. He's a tough old bird, he'll be all right."

Fargo nodded toward a bundled-up mackinaw now resting on the hard ground. "But he won't. That's the body of Orrin Lofley, a cooper from Mormon Station. Killed north of here."

Saunders nodded, his face grim. Ultimately, these deaths rested on his shoulders, and he felt the burden terribly.

"Utes, right?" he said. "Command keeps banging my ears about these infernal grogshops. I agree they have to go, but whoever's behind them is clever. When soldiers show up, the shops reappear elsewhere. And there's never any still discovered—that's hidden somewhere very secure."

The doc had already tended to Winslowe and was now applying his stethoscope to Estelline, with the kids waiting their turn. The soldiers were behaving as courteously and professionally as the physician. The Mormon Battalion was founded, at President Polk's request, to help General Kearney conquer California. They earned an excellent battle record and had remained active to defend Deseret.

"You're right, Utes wounded Winslowe," Fargo said. "But I'd bet a gold cartwheel it was Dill Stover who killed Orrin—meaning to hit me."

"Stover! That cur? Everybody's touting him as the sure winner of the Salt Lake Run coming up in only a few days. Unless, of course, you and your stallion are in the race."

Fargo ignored the last remark. "Well, if he's in the race, then tell me this—have you seen Stover in Salt Lake lately?" he demanded.

Saunders removed his plumed hat, thinking. "Actually, no."

"That's because he's been too busy throwing lead at us. Another tip: Frederic Childress and Cecil McGinnis will be in town for the race. Might pay to watch those two. Watch 'em close—especially if you're serious about ending these Indian troubles."

"Childress, huh?" Saunders paused, then added: "He's Dill Stover's latest employer, right?"

Fargo grinned. "Now you're using your think-piece, soldier. And he's behind the grogshops as well as the one who's stirring up the Indians and the Indian haters."

Saunders was so astonished his strong jaw fell open. "Damn! I can't believe it, Skye! Childress is forever preaching the 'progressive' line about Indians."

"Yeah, he preaches the sweet lavender in public. But in secret, or among remote groups in the outposts, he's hotjawin' the Indians, including with broadsheets McGinnis prints up. He's trying to push things to a shooting war. Even tried to hire me to help him out."

Saunders still looked flabbergasted, but he knew Fargo too well to question his judgment.

"That slimy hypocrite," the officer said slowly. "You know what? He'll be speaking on 'Indian relations' Saturday after next at the Civic Lecture Hall. I remember that because security is going to be tight, his being gentile and all. There'll be plenty of our soldiers."

"Ahem."

Both men glanced over at Dora.

"Skye," she said pointedly, "Saturday after next is August tenth."

Fargo got her point, but chose to ignore it.

"Dora, this is Captain Saunders Lee," he said to change the subject.

"Well, hell-*oh* there, Captain," she greeted the handsome young officer flirtatiously.

Fargo grinned when Saunders gave her only a curt nod. *Good luck, lady,* Fargo thought. Saunders Lee was the most no-nonsense, duty-bound man he'd ever met.

By now the doctor had finished and the travelers were ready for the final, brief leg into Salt Lake City under military escort. Orrin Lofley's body was taken up by a soldier, and John drove the oxen in place of the wounded Elder Winslowe. Fargo rode out front beside Saunders, the desert heat heavy on his back and shoulders. The horses held a fast walk, the best pace the oxen could keep.

"Well . . . are you?" Saunders demanded.

Fargo turned his face toward the officer, though his slanted brim left half of it in shadow. "Am I what?"

"Fargo, that poker face of yours never did fool me. You know damn well what I mean. Are you entering the Salt Lake Run, you muttonhead?"

"Oh, that. Yeah, I'm told there's some discussion of that subject in these parts," Fargo said with evident sarcasm.

"That's drawing it mild, friend. It's the leading question in town—will Fargo enter his Ovaro? Even folks who've never heard of you or your horse are placing bets."

Fargo grinned, but from habit his eyes stayed in constant motion. "Kinda odds they giving me?"

"Frankly," Saunders admitted, "not the best. Not with Dill Stover and his roan in the race."

Fargo nodded. "That horse is probably stolen, like the new saddle, but Stover does take good care of it, I'll grant that."

"Stover is a drunkard and a braggart," Saunders said. "And he's gotten away with murdering Indians in cold blood. But he's a good rider. And good is all you need to be on a horse like his."

"Wait a minute here," Fargo said. He nodded toward Saunders's big gray gelding. "That's a fine-looking animal, and you were always the boy for a race yourself. But you're not in it?"

His friend frowned deeply, revealing feelings of resentment and disappointment. Saunders glanced behind to make sure his men wouldn't hear him complaining.

"Skye, I wanted a chance at this race bad," he confessed. "But I can't enter because I'll be in charge of security. Besides the cash prize, the winner gets a lucrative mail contract."

"Yeah, but why would you care? You're a career officer."

"Was. I want to resign my commission."

It was Fargo's turn to look astounded. "You, with all that heels together and keep up the strut? You swore you'd die in the saddle."

"That was before I met a woman."

This time Fargo almost fell out of the saddle. "A woman, for God's sake? Captain Ramrod Spine himself, master of self-denial?"

"Head over heels in love," Saunders admitted. "But she's an outlander, so it'll ruin me in the Mormon community if I marry her. That's why I wanted to win that mail contract. It's federal as well as territorial. Those jobs can be held by non-Mormons. We could be rich in several years, move anywhere we choose."

Fargo nodded. "Who's the gal?"

"I best not say yet. It could get rough for her *and* me. Tell you the truth, I haven't even said much to her about how I feel. What's the point until I can do something about it?"

Fargo lapsed into silence as they rode ever closer to Salt Lake City, nestled among irrigated fields. He thought about the upcoming race in the intimidating saline wastes west of the city, the desolate heart of the Great Salt Lake Desert. It was a boiling inferno at this time of year and the footing was treacherous thanks to unstable blow sand.

"You may get that mail contract anyway," Fargo finally told his friend. "If I win the race, I'll sell it to you for one dollar. I don't want the damn thing, it's too close to a job."

"So you *are* entering the race?"

"Yeah, for my sins. I'd rather have longer than three days to rest up the Ovaro—not quite three, actually. But he's not been pushed hard, at least. Besides, I'm anxious to meet up with old Dill anyway, so I think I'll enter."

"It's one hundred twenty hardscrabble miles," Saunders

reminded him. "Absolutely no shade the entire course. No maps or other navigational aids permitted. You've been out there—there's no reference points of any kind. Just the sun, the horizon lines, and later the night sky."

Fargo lifted a shoulder. "It'll be a rough piece of work, all right. But I can use that two hundred fifty dollar purse. And if I do manage to win, that keeps the mail contract out of Stover's hands. Assuming he survives the race, that is."

Saunders sent him a sidelong glance. "Think he might not?"

"Distinct possibility one of us won't," Fargo predicted.

"So that's the way it is?"

"That's the way it is," Fargo agreed. "By the way, where will I be staying?"

"You'll have your usual room at Emmerick's boarding-house. Esther was tickled to reserve it for you when I asked, even though she called you a 'sunken sinner.'"

Saunders's remark suddenly made it occur to Fargo, whose thoughts had been otherwise occupied lately, that his enemies needn't wait until he was out in the open desert again. Childress, McGinnis, and Stover would all be in Salt Lake City, and it wasn't difficult to figure out where out-landers were staying.

Deseret's big hero, Saunders had jokingly called him. Fargo had always feared that label. Every time it got stuck on him, hot lead always followed.

10

Despite his wound, Elder Winslowe insisted on getting the Beckmann family and Dora comfortably settled as soon as the little convoy of soldiers and civilians reached Salt Lake City by midmorning. Using his official status as a church elder, he declared them destitute transients, and thus immediately eligible for Mormon aid. They were assigned a pleasant house on Seventh Street.

While they settled in, Fargo headed for the livery stable on the western outskirts of town, right next door to Emmerick's boardinghouse. He was astonished at the change in Salt Lake City, most of it occasioned by the upcoming race.

The Utah Territory, as Deseret formally became in 1850, had been forced to endure gentiles as their government officers, but it was unusual to see so many non-Mormons strolling in the streets on holiday. True, come dark most would be forced to sleep in camps at the edge of the city. But clean camps with water and firewood provided.

A hot air balloon was tethered to a wooden stand beside City Creek. Many buildings, in this normally plain and simple, God-fearing town, now sported red-white-and-blue bunting. Fargo even spotted a few beer tents. Rustic outlanders, some wearing coyote-skin caps, prowled the streets under the watchful eyes of polite but vigilant soldiers.

It was good to again see a few saloons with sawdust-covered floors. But the honky-tonk gals were conspicuously absent—fornication was illegal in Salt Lake City and not to be encouraged by any means.

"Still two days and a wake-up before the race," Fargo remarked to his stallion, "and the place already looks like

Fourth of July. That means big betting—and big betting means big trouble.''

The Ovaro, who was still a little flighty in this busy city traffic after weeks in the vast emptiness of the desert, snorted and pricked up his ears as if agreeing.

"You're getting the royal treatment between now and the race, old campaigner," Fargo added. "Two days with Micajah Jones."

Fargo tugged rein and they trotted through the open pole gate of a thriving livery. An old man straight out of Genesis was working a blindfolded coyote dun on a breaking pole, and controlling it with apparent ease.

"Micajah, you *are* a horse," Fargo greeted him.

Micajah rarely bothered with greetings. "And *you*, by grab, are a horse's ass, Skye, if you think two days rest is enough before that stallion runs this weekend."

Fargo grinned as he swung down and dropped the bridle, letting the Ovaro drink from a stone trough.

"I know, old-timer, you're right. But that's why I came to you. If anybody can work a horse into top fettle fast, it's you. All set for the big weekend?"

The old man grunted. "Air ye daft, lad? I wouldn't give a plug nickel for the whole shivaree. I despise a horse race, I truly do."

Micajah was already working the Ovaro's sore shoulder muscles with gnarled but deft hands.

"Suffering Moses," the hostler said with true reverence. "*That's* horseflesh."

Micajah moved slowly around the Ovaro, studying him with an expert's eye.

"Most white men these days," he said, "won't ride an uncut stallion like you and Injins do. They claim gelding makes a horse easier to control around the mares. Mebbe so, but a gelded horse will always lose bottom in a hard run. On account it's been spirit-broke."

Fargo nodded sincere agreement. Breaking a horse to leather, the white man's way, involved choking, water-starving, and using wire bits that cut the horse's mouth when it rebelled. Of course such treatment broke the spirit. And like a man, a horse *needed* spirit.

No horse of Skye Fargo's had ever known a breaking saddle. He broke them in the same way the great horse tribes in the short-grass country did—he simply jumped on and rode until the horse was exhausted. If he was still on when the animal finally stopped, Fargo was the master.

"Dill Stover rides a gelded horse," Fargo remarked as he stripped off his saddle, blanket, and pad. "Would you call his roan spirit-broke, too?"

He gratefully accepted a jug of mash and set it on his shoulder while Micajah considered the question.

"That roan," the old man finally answered, "is a broken drum—it can't be beat. Sure, the horse has been cut. Been broke to leather the white man's way, too. Hell yes, it's a mite spirit-broke. But it just don't matter, dang garn it, that hoss is one in ten thousand. Got Arabian blood mixed with original Spanish stock. Arabians take to desert like ducks to water. Your stallion was mountain born and bred."

"Well, I asked," Fargo said on a sigh. "I think my stallion can beat the roan."

Micajah nodded. "Mebbe. You're a better rider. Happens it's a fair race, you'll stand a fighting chance. But with all the legem pone I hear Fred Childress has got riding on Stover's roan, the race'll be crooked—and I don't mean the shape of the course."

"So I'm not the only one in Deseret who doesn't trust Childress?"

"The big boss," Micajah said, meaning Brigham Young, "don't know beans from buckshot about human character. I can't prove it, but that Childress is a snake. This Saturday, you cover your ampersand, Skye, hear? Keep eyes in the back of your head."

Carrying his saddle, Fargo walked next door to the sprawling boardinghouse. He was given a ground-floor room at the back of the dwelling, next to the kitchen. It was small but comfortable, with a chintz-covered chest, a wash stand, and a towel rack. A Mormon Bible sat conspicuously atop a little escritoire beside the narrow iron bedstead.

Fargo cleaned up, then left on foot to find the registration tent so he could officially enter the race. He searched all the faces he passed, but didn't spot Stover, Childress, or McGinnis. Nonetheless, Fargo felt like the bull's-eye on a target, a feeling he was getting damned tired of.

He returned to the boardinghouse and followed a downstairs hallway to the back of the building. He nodded at a drummer carrying a straw sample case, who was just emerging from the room next to his.

"In town for the race, friend?" the drummer called out after Skye.

"You got it in one," Fargo told him.

That was all the invitation the drummer needed. He shook open his case quick as snapping a finger. "In that case, friend, you'll require an excellent, yet inexpensive, spyglass—"

"Maybe later," Fargo cut him short. "Right now time's pushing."

The drummer nodded and left. Fargo was about to key the lock when he heard a noise from inside, a sound like drawers being rapidly opened and shut.

He shucked out his Colt and thumb-cocked it. Then he flung open the unlocked door.

"Oh!"

The young woman rifling drawers shot up straight, spun around, then gaped in wide-eyed terror at the blued steel clutched in his fist. She wore the apron and coif of a maid or cleaning woman. But that pretty white dress with the lace collar seemed too elegantly cut for a Mormon woman.

"Something I could help you find?" Fargo greeted her, admiring her liquid green eyes. They shimmered in the light slanting through a sash window beside the bed.

"Help me?—" The young woman's laugh sounded a bit forced, to Fargo. "Of course not, Mr. Fargo. My name is Lily, I work here. I was just making sure you have everything you need."

"Lily, huh? Pretty name. Well, Lily, a man never has *everything* he needs."

"Maybe he could if he just asked."

Her one-second transformation, from startled innocent to sultry wanton, made Fargo laugh so hard he had to punch his thigh. Some women thought they could pull off anything simply by dazzling a man with some flesh. He blocked the door so she couldn't leave.

"When a good-looking woman like you," he said, crossing the room toward her, "offers to give her favors away that quick, she's got something to hide."

She backed nervously away, trying to distract him. "Something to hide? How silly. So . . . I hear you've seen the elephant?"

"And the monkey and the giraffe, too. So what?"

Only now, as he drew up before the defiant woman, did Fargo make the connection: like the supposed image seen in Dora's "peeping stone" she had red hair.

Dora's voice pricked at him: *She's real, Skye, and on August tenth, just nine days from today, something terrible happens to her.*

"Plenty of women have red hair," he muttered, plunging a hand in her dress pocket and fishing out a Colt Pocket Model.

"*Give* me that!" she protested, trying to snatch it from him. The ensuing wrestling match, which he won, turned into an erotic grapple that left both of them breathing hard, and not from exertion.

"All right, Lily," Fargo said, dropping the gun back in her pocket after removing the cartridges. "I understand a woman having a gun. But carrying it with her inside the house where she works? That's tangle-brained. Salt Lake isn't exactly a wide-open heller."

"In case you haven't noticed, Mr. Far—"

"Skye."

"In case you haven't noticed, Skye, I'm considered a comely woman. And this is a boardinghouse filled with unmarried men."

"Right on both counts," he conceded.

Her lucent green eyes softened. "My defensive attitude, however, is different if the male advances are welcome."

Fargo's eyes raked over her. "I've made no advances . . . yet."

"No, you haven't, have you?"

"You're no Mormon," Fargo said. "So why are you here?"

The story she told was familiar enough. Two years before, her husband, Jimmy, had died on the California Trail. The Mormons took her in, but only for menial labor. Her life now was one of constant work with no social life.

"If you find it so unpleasant," Fargo said, "why not leave? You're not a prisoner here, you could join a wagon train headed east or west."

"Lilian!" screeched a female voice from the front of the house. "Lilian, confound it, where are you?"

"Oh, criminy! That's Esther," Lily exclaimed, hurrying toward the door. "I best go or she'll skin me alive."

She paused at the door to glance back at him. "I haven't been with a man since my husband died. And not too many like you come through here. Would you object to company later?"

Fargo grinned. But then he suddenly recalled what Saunders had told him about a gentile woman he hoped to marry. How many could there be in Salt Lake City?

"You're not by any chance promised to a Mormon?" he asked.

"Not likely."

"Is one even sparking you?" he pressed.

"Not even calling on me," she assured him.

Fargo's grin reappeared. But later he would turn this situation over and examine all of its facets. Lily was holding something back.

"Sure," he finally told her, "I'd like company later."

As a member in good standing of the church (to all appearances), newspaperman Cecil McGinnis owned a house on Poplar Street near the college. He, Frederic Childress, and Dill Stover met there at the same time Fargo was talking to the mysterious Lily Snyder.

"All your feeble excuses won't feed the bulldog, Dill," Childress said with cold, angry precision. "This is multiple failures now. Once or twice, all right, that could be chance events. But what we have now is a clear pattern of bungling."

The three men had retreated into a private den where the servants couldn't eavesdrop.

"Well, your precious goddamn Indians ain't done no better," Stover reminded his employer.

"Never mind the Utes. *You* presented yourself to us, Dill, as a fearless and rugged man of action, a former army scout and combat veteran. In fact, however, all Cecil and I see is a calamity howler who spends his time finding reasons for not acting."

"Aw, horseshit. It's just—"

Childress waved him quiet. "Horseshit is precisely the

word. All you've been doing, this past week, is washing bricks. If Fargo frightens you, just say so, man! We'll send you packing and hire a man that owns a pair."

"You're *way* off the trail now," Stover protested, unable to take his eyes off a decanter of liquor on a nearby table. "Fargo's just damn good at staying above the ground, is all."

"That's *all*?" Childress swore quietly, rose from his chair, paced the room. His pale-agate eyes were reptilian in the afternoon light slanting through the curtains.

His continued silence made Stover nervous. He feared being fired, but also figured Childress wouldn't give him the boot now, with so much money bet on him for the race. And if Stover won, he'd be on good terms again with his employers.

"It's those damned red Arabs, I'm telling you," he carped again. "They don't care a hoot in hell about killing Fargo. All they could think about, on the trip down, was snatching them women and kids and selling them to the slave traders in New Mex."

"They're ignorant savages, Dill. The hell's *your* excuse?" Childress snapped.

"Perhaps Dill does have something of a point," McGinnis interceded smoothly, his specialty. "They say an empty hand is no lure for a hawk, Frederic. True, we give them rifles and liquor. But maybe the other gimcracks and gewgaws we offer the Indians are not enough incentive. All those ribbons and medals and bright baubles."

Childress considered that. "Well, a few glass beads bought Manhattan. But I'll talk to them later about it. They're standing by west of the city. He Bear was winged by Fargo this morning, but it's not serious enough to put him out of action. They're both waiting for later, when they'll join Dill for tonight's attack that *will* kill Fargo."

Stover's blunt jaw dropped open. "Right in town?"

"Of course, it's ideal. Look at the potential suspects what with all these visitors in town for the race. Including outlanders, whom Mormons suspect on principle. The taverns are even open later, putting crowds and noise in the streets."

"But, hell, what if the place where he's staying—"

"See?" Childress demanded. "See it? Always making excuses not to act. Look, we know exactly where Fargo is staying, Emmerick's boardinghouse on Commerce Street. It's that big frame wood place on the edge of town next to the livery. It'll be a cinch for the Utes to slip in after dark and join you."

"Them stinking fleabags?" Stover grumped. "Put them inside a house with civilized people, the smell will give us away."

"There's the beauty of it," Childress told him. "You won't *need* to go inside. I have spies everywhere. Fargo is in room number four, which is on the ground floor at the back of the house—*with* a window. It's all open grass lot back there. The bed is right in front of the window—I want the three of you to pour massed firepower through that window. Then run like hell."

Stover looked unsure, his heavy brows almost touching. "You sure this is a smart play, Mr. Childress? It'll be a helluva racket when the three of us burn powder."

"It's only noise, and noise never convicted a man. Dill, for Christ sakes, it'll be a lot easier and smarter to kill Fargo in his room than to worry about it this Saturday on the racecourse."

"If he's killed on the course," McGinnis pitched in, for Stover still looked unconvinced, "it looks much more suspicious for all of us, what with the heavy betting on you. And if we fail on Saturday, and Fargo wins, there goes a mail contract worth thousands. Best not to take the chance."

"Right now," Childress added, "is an especially awkward time to have a crusader like Fargo in Salt Lake City. The military command is starting to come around on the issue of replacing their old single-shot Hall rifles with repeaters. That's a fifteen thousand dollar order plus another five thousand dollars for ammunition."

Childress paused until Stover met his eyes. "So to hell with the noise, Dill, pour in a *wall* of lead! There's personal fortunes at stake here, including your own. In the absence of laws, blatant violence is the most effective approach. I saw it work firsthand in the tong wars out in San Francisco."

"All right," Stover said. "Just answer me this: Who saves my bacon when Fargo's avengers start looking for justice? He's famous now, a big man."

"I pay one councilman," Childress insisted, "and there *is* no investigation."

Stover nodded and stood up. He had his own room right in the house and wanted to get back to it—and his bottle.

"That's all I needed to hear," Stover said. "Those Indians ain't got the mentality for nothing fancy. But it don't take no smarts to unlimber through a window. Later tonight we'll paper the walls with Fargo's brains."

The Trailsman spent some of the afternoon swapping thoughts with Saunders, especially regarding Frederic Childress and Cecil McGinnis. They also discussed and studied the 120-mile race course in detail, relying on a map of the Great Salt Lake Desert that Fargo himself helped draw.

Then Fargo visited the Beckmanns and Dora in their temporary home on Seventh Street. They were already snugly moved in, and Fargo stayed for a delicious supper of roast beef, potatoes, and fresh greens.

"Leaving so soon?" Dora complained when Fargo grabbed his hat off the sideboard soon after supper. "I thought you might like to see my new room?"

Her inviting tone tempted Fargo, but he resisted.

"Darlin'," he advised, "think real careful before you take a man into your room. This is Salt Lake City, you're not married, and spies are everywhere. The wrong story gets reported, you folks could be out of a house. And Estelline's near ready to foal."

Dora frowned. "I know you're right. Should I wear ashes and sackcloth, too?"

"That wouldn't help, you'd still look pretty. Just be very discreet."

Fargo felt a little guilt as he walked back to the boardinghouse in the grainy twilight. He'd meant what he told Dora. Nonetheless, he was hoping to do, later on tonight, exactly what he'd cautioned Dora against: fornication.

Fargo was able to get to his room without the usual small talk because many of the tenants were still seated at the huge dining room table. Once inside his room, he thumb-scratched a lucifer into flame and lit the lamp, turning up the wick.

He cleaned and loaded both his weapons, reminding himself to buy more ammo tomorrow. Fargo also conned over this new problem named Lily. A beautiful, redheaded problem. She never did explain why she was still here so long after her husband died—that made no sense. What did this place have to hold her?

Nor did her toting a gun in law-abiding Salt Lake City make much sense. Unless . . . unless her story was all a lie? And there was that soft-brained foolishness of Dora's, that hokum about August tenth and a "beautiful redhead drenched in blood." Fargo didn't believe in such claptrap, of course, but a few more questions might be in order.

Thinking all this, listening to the rhythm of insects through the open window, Fargo blew out the lamp, stripped down to his cotton drawers, and enjoyed the feel of crawling between crisp, clean sheets. For a moment he remembered that he had meant to move his bed away from the window. But already his eyelids felt weighted with coins, and sleep rapidly embraced him.

"Skye! Skye, *please* open up before someone catches me!"

The whisper was low, yet urgent enough to have woken him. Fargo heard a scratching noise at the door. He snapped awake and came up on one elbow. The position and color of the moon told him it was well past midnight. The muslin curtains fluttered in the window as a cool breeze filled the room.

"Hold on," he whispered, relying on moonlight to guide him across the room to the door.

Fargo tugged her quickly inside, for the hallway was lighted by candles in brass wall sconces. She wore only a chenille robe, and it was on the floor before he had the door locked. Lily pressed against him, her hand playing pleasant games inside his drawers.

"It's been so long, Skye," she whispered. "This was worth the risk," she added, giving his curving manhood a squeeze. "Now let's put the stud through his facings."

He pulled her into bed with him, the moonlight tracing her statuesque body with its hard, pointy breasts, long and shapely thighs, and flaring hips divided by a silky vee of mons hair. Her lush red hair, almost the same shade as russet leaves, fanned out against his stomach as she began taking exploratory licks up and down his shaft.

"The lack of practice hasn't hurt you," he assured her between groans of pleasure.

While she treated him with her mouth, Fargo slid one hand up those long, slim, supple thighs until he found the wet and furry nest at their apex. Lily began adding her groans to his. She rubbed against his hand with fast and urgent swipes, leaving his fingers damp with her desire.

"Oh, I . . . I feel it building, Skye!" she whispered excitedly. "Here it . . . *oh*! Skye, *oh* my goodness, NOW!"

His busy hand teased her to a shuddering climax. By now she had Fargo primed for release, and he settled between her splayed-open thighs, flexing his buttocks to open and enter the hot, slippery, velvet sheath that she eagerly began moving in a perfect rhythm with his thrusting manhood.

"Skye!" she gasped, shudder after shudder moving over her. "My God, you fill me so completely! Oh, *oh* yes, do that! Yes, *that*! Oh, please, swirl it again . . . *oh*!"

Hating to dampen her fire, but not wanting to see Lily get in serious trouble, Fargo said, "Easy, hon, not so loud. It's not just gossip we risk."

"Sorry!"

She quieted down for a few minutes, but soon she was keening with pleasure and clawing Fargo's back as both of them exploded in powerful release. Spent and exhausted, they lay in a lazy daze for uncounted minutes. Now and then the breeze stiffened, pleasantly goose-pimpling Fargo's bare flesh but also reminding him of something he'd meant to do before sleep overtook him.

The windswept muslin curtains licked at his legs and he remembered—he'd meant to move the bed. There was a window over it and a big, open lot behind it.

"That was nice, Skye," Lily murmured beside him. "Take all you want, there's plenty more."

Fargo ignored her, muscles tensing. Early during his training as a scout and tracker, Fargo had learned a crucial lesson that had since saved his life more than once: *be careful when the insects suddenly fall silent.*

As they had just done outside the window.

"Skye?" Lily said when he bolted up in bed, "what's the—*hey*!"

Fargo embraced her, all right, but only so that he could roll out of bed fast and hard, slamming to the floor.

"Skye? What—"

"Just stay down," he hissed even as he crammed her under the bed and squeezed in with her as far as he could, hoping that mattress was a thick one.

"Skye Fargo! This is—Jesus!"

The window glass exploded inward as a hammering racket of gunfire—rifle and handgun—shattered the calm night. Shards of glass sprayed Fargo's exposed limbs, and plaster dust spouted in white geysers as bullets pockmarked the wall behind him.

The unlit lantern exploded, filling the room with the stench of kerosene; the porcelain washbowl shattered; the pillows coughed feathers as slugs ripped into them; a round penetrated the thin flock wall and whanged off the iron cookstove in the adjoining kitchen.

Just as suddenly as it began, the furious volley stopped. Fargo heard running feet retreating across the empty lot.

Lily had gone fear-simple. "Oh-my-god, oh-my-god, oh-my-god," she kept repeating.

Fargo tugged her carefully out, avoiding the jagged shards of glass, and gently slapped her.

"Nerve up, girl, you're all right. Quick, get your robe on and get back to your room—"

The hallway door suddenly banged open, and lantern light flooded the room. Hiram Emmerick stood there with a double-ten express gun aimed inward. Behind him, craning her neck for a better view, was his shocked wife, Esther. A hallway full of residents pressed in behind them.

Fargo and Lily stood there naked as newborns. The window, frame and all, was completely blown out and the glass had been sprayed everywhere. The mattress and walls were shot to smithereens, and the stench of spent powder was overwhelming.

Overcome at the shocking and sinful sight, Esther Emmerick swooned.

"Howdy, folks," Fargo called out cheerfully. "Can I get you anything?"

94

11

Lily recovered enough presence of mind to hastily fling on her robe. Fargo, figuring there was no point in hurrying now, plucked his buckskin trousers off a nail on the wall and stepped into them.

"Folks," he suggested calmly, "not much more to see. Several attackers opened fire through the window. Now it's a matter for the law."

At his hint a few of the gawkers did peel off from the group and return to their rooms. However, there were more faces squeezing into the doorway than leaving it.

"I can't even get out of here," Lily hissed in his ear, embarrassed and frustrated. "That doorway's packed tight, and the hallway, too. We're on view in a cage."

"Lilian Snyder!" shrieked Esther, who'd been brought around by smelling salts. Her prim, angry face looked ridiculous under a long and striped sleeping cap. "Or is Lily only your name *this* summer, strumpet?"

"What would you expect from a godless outlander?" demanded a scowling, bearded man with a pinched face. His eyes slid from Lily to Fargo. "After all, if one oak bears acorns, all oaks will."

"If you got some feeble point you're trying to make," Fargo invited him, "no need to chew it so fine."

"I'm not a gunman."

"Then maybe," Fargo suggested, his eyes piercing the man like a pair of bullets, "you should stop making insults you don't have the spine to back up."

Esther, however, reserved most of her outrage for Lily, not Fargo.

"I'm half a mind," she exploded at the "fallen" young

woman, "to put you out on the street right this instant, you wanton little hussy."

Fargo had noticed an odd fact about women: they were far harsher, in their condemnation of their sisters, than men were.

"Now, now, Esther," intervened Elder West, "you'll do no such thing. Remember your Christian charity."

"Ours is the stern God of Moses," she insisted.

"Also a *thrifty* God," Hiram reminded his wife. "Your 'outrage' is fine, but who's going to pay for all this damage?"

"Tell you the straight, Hiram," Fargo said, "the damage *should* be paid by the jackasses who did it."

"Your being here," Esther snapped, "is what lured the jackasses."

"Now, Esther, be fair," Elder West admonished. "This is the same man who has done so much for our people. As you yourself were just saying not long ago."

"Well . . ." The old matriarch's face did soften a bit. "He has been a champion for us, hasn't he? I apologize to Mr. Fargo."

"Wait a minute!" protested the pinch-faced man. "Nothing against Fargo. But our law was violated here tonight. Surely it must be reported to the city police?"

"The shooting attack must be, of course," Elder West said. "As for the other . . . why bother?"

"Why *bother*?"

"Exactly. It's a waste of time, and we Mormons are a practical lot. Arresting Skye Fargo, 'the Deseret Scout,' on such a minor charge is out of the question. Especially with the race coming up day after tomorrow. Actually," he corrected himself, glancing at his gold watch, "coming up tomorrow."

The Elder's eyes cut to Lily. Her face was defiant, but she was so ashamed she stared at the glass-strewn floor.

"As for Lily," he went on, "she's in very little official trouble. After all, what occurred here tonight did not involve a Latter-day Saint of either sex. No need to overreact—we are not moral police for the outlanders."

As a peace offering, Fargo paid for the damage even though it cleaned out his cash supply. With that the Emmericks finally went back to bed. The rest followed suit.

When Lily started to leave, Elder West detained her.

"Child," he said kindly, "don't live in fear of Esther's vengeance. I have a great deal of influence with her, and she is obedient to the churchmen. I will tell her I dealt with the matter. For the time being, however, I suggest you refrain from your duties around here."

"Don't worry. Right now I'd like to crawl into a hole and pull the hole in after me."

West glanced at Fargo. "What you two've done is still a violation of law, of course. I do hope you'll refrain while here. But, after all . . ."

He looked at the striking redhead and smiled wistfully. "You're *only* a man, Skye Fargo, made of flesh and all it's heir to."

"Amen," Fargo said piously, winking at Lily.

"And frankly," West said as he headed out the door, "I envy you."

Lily started for the door, too.

"See?" Fargo said behind her. "He's a good sort."

She turned around and nodded, her face thoughtful and troubled. "He is, isn't he?"

"Damn, girl, why does that seem to trouble you?"

But she was already gone, and again Fargo had a nettlesome thought about pretty redheads, August tenth, and "peeping stones."

At first, as Fargo stewed on the violent attempt tonight, he got mad as a badger in a barrel. By his count this was the sixth attempt to kill him in as many days. But he quickly calmed down to a cool, lethal sense of purpose. After all, he wasn't encumbered with an emigrant family to nursemaid anymore. And it was his way to return a visit as soon as possible.

First, however, he needed to formally prove what he already knew: who his attackers were.

Fargo finished dressing in the dark and strapped on his thick leather gun belt. Grabbing his Henry, he stepped out through the shattered window to the moonlit lot.

"Lot" was a misnomer. After a few dozen yards of sparse, tufted grass, the yard simply gave way to open desert. Carefully, Fargo knelt under the windowsill to study the ground.

Even in the pale yellow moonlight he could easily see brass shell casings everywhere. The grass stopped about a foot from the building, and by peering very close Fargo could make out three separate sets of prints, two of them made by moccasins, the third by boots with a cross cut in the heels. Those crosscut boots were army issue, and Fargo had seen the prints several times during the journey to Salt Lake City.

"Two Utes and Dill Stover," Fargo muttered as he stood back up. "Strange bedfellows."

By now it was closer to dawn than midnight, but Fargo had his belly full of these stinking sage rats and he wanted to retaliate while they were feeling safe from it. He followed the tracks out into the desert. Fargo found the place where they had hobbled their mounts, only one of which was shod.

The Indian ponies had gone straight out into the desert. The shod horse, however, had angled around to enter town on Poplar Street.

Where, he already knew from talking to Saunders Lee earlier, Cecil McGinnis owned a home—a home where Fred Childress always stayed when in Salt Lake City.

Fargo slipped along under the rustling poplars and cedars, occasionally spotting a scavenging wolf slink through the shadows. When he drew abreast of the two-story stone house at 722 Poplar, he slipped into the big side yard and around back.

A small stable was locked, and Fargo decided not to risk agitating Stover's horse, and waking the men, simply to verify the roan was inside. It was enough proof when Fargo found the prints of crosscut boots all over the yard.

A large shed sat at the back of the property. Fargo knew that Childress and McGinnis wouldn't be reckless enough to keep a still there. But he used his Arkansas Toothpick to pry several planks loose from the back wall and squeeze inside. A fast search, by the light of several matches, turned up a carefully hidden box of broadsheets spreading the anti-Indian message. Fargo took one, folded it, stuck it in his pocket.

Even though the boot prints proved, to Fargo's satisfaction, that Stover was with the Utes earlier tonight, Fargo intended to take his retaliation right to the man who hired out all his killings, the man who charged dying travelers fifteen dollars for a glass of water—Frederic Childress, who was asleep right now in one room of this house.

But Fargo meant to make sure.

It was easy enough to spot the servants' wing in the rear, next to the clotheslines and washtubs. Fargo picked the first open window and, after listening a moment, crawled inside. He aimed toward the sound of soft breathing, seeing the dim outline of a white-clad form.

Fargo felt for the bedside candle, touched a match to the wick. The sleeper in the bed was a middle-aged woman with coarse-grained skin and the rough, raw hands of a scrubwoman.

The light caused her eyes to start fluttering open. Fargo quickly placed a hand over her mouth.

"*Don't* be scared, ma'am," he whispered. "I know it's shocking as hell to wake up to a strange man in your room. But if I meant to harm you, I'd've done it by now, right?"

Fargo expected hysterics. But after her initial surprise, the woman calmed right down. She nodded to indicate her cooperation.

"You're not a strange man," she gainsaid when he cautiously removed his hand from her mouth. "You're Skye Fargo, the Trailsman. Saw your likeness in the newspaper, though it doesn't do those blue eyes justice. I feel honored. My name is Regina, by the way."

Fargo grinned. For once his damned notoriety was beneficial.

"Regina, honored to meet you. So you work for Cecil McGinnis?"

She nodded, moving over so Fargo could perch on one side of the bed. "My husband died of double hernia and I had to find work. I'm the laundress and the cook's assistant."

"You like working for McGinnis?"

Her eyes fled from Fargo's.

"What, does he mistreat you, Regina?"

"No," she answered reluctantly. "He's usually up at Mormon Station, anyway, with his newspaper. He's quite lenient with his servants."

"Then why is it," Fargo pressed, "that as soon as I mentioned him, you looked like you smelled a sewer leaking?"

"Mr. Fargo, I was back in Illinois in the 1840s when the anti-Mormons burned us out of Nauvoo. McGinnis claims to be Mormon, but the men with whom he associates are no different than those who burned us out."

"Men," Fargo clarified, "like Frederic Childress and Dill Stover?"

"To name the very devils, yessir. They're both asleep under this roof right now. That heathen Stover! The last time he was here in town he beat up an old farmer and shot a chandelier down at the Grand Mesa Saloon. But McGinnis went bond for him, following the orders of Childress. Stover ought to have been horsewhipped and driven into the desert."

"He requires something more permanent than that," Fargo said quietly.

"Then give it to him. No man is more deserving except for Childress."

Fargo quickly found out which three bedrooms the men occupied. He warned Regina that bedlam was about to erupt, but that the servants would all be safe. He didn't bother asking her not to tell anyone about his visit—his enemies were hell-bent on killing him, not on turning him over to the law, so it didn't matter who knew he was here.

Fargo slipped back outside, then went round to the opposite side of the house. That middle pair of windows, according to Regina, would be Childress's room. Fargo had no intention of aiming to kill, just spraying the room. But if Childress got in the way of some lead, to hell with him. Let the bastard eat what he dished out.

The window to the right was McGinnis's room, and Stover should pose no threat—he'd been relegated to the servants' wing. Besides, he was "drunk as the lords of Creation," in Regina's phrase.

Fargo jacked a round into the chamber of the Henry and cautiously edged closer to the window in the predawn stillness. He was critically low on ammo, so his plan was to empty all sixteen rounds from the Henry and hold his Colt in reserve in case he had to blast his way out.

The pair of windows was open, lace curtains billowing out. Fargo crouched, fired from the hip, then followed on with a rapid-fire burst that shattered the peaceful night. He deliberately aimed high to destroy the raised glass and grinned with grim satisfaction when a mirror, too, shattered within.

"Stop it!" screamed the terrified voice of Frederic Childress. "Christ Almighty, *stop* it!"

"How's it feel, you son of a bitch?" Fargo muttered, still levering and firing.

The window on the right had not seriously concerned Fargo. McGinnis was an ink-slinger, not a gunslinger. He regretted that assumption, however, the very moment muzzle flame leaped through the darkness toward him.

Fargo had just emptied the Henry, and Childress was literally whimpering from within. The moment he heard the shot behind him, Fargo whirled, drew steel, and blasted away at the window.

"Stop, I'm wounded!" cried the reedy voice of McGinnis. "I surrender!"

You'll surrender in hell, all three of you, Fargo promised as he melted away into the shadows.

Lily did return to her room, after her public humiliation downstairs, but sleep was out of the question. She dressed in dark clothing, making sure she had her gun. Then she left the boardinghouse by rear outside stairs seldom used by the guests.

Sticking to the blue-black shadows, she hurried toward the Civic Lecture Hall as she had so many times before. Skye Fargo, she told herself, was a wonderful lover, all right, albeit a dangerous man to spend time with. Nonetheless, she now regretted giving in to temptation. It meant she would be punished even more harshly after her "sensational crime" coming up next weekend.

Eight days now, she thought with a little sting of nervousness. *Exactly one week after their precious race tomorrow.*

She entered the big wooden building by a rear door and took the stairs to the attic, familiar with every inch of it. Not until she slid the entrance panel off the crawlspace did she need to light a candle.

"Lord, steady my hand next Saturday," she murmured as she surveyed the little cubbyhole she'd prepared for the purpose of dealing ultimate justice to Frederic Childress. The distance was not daunting, for she had practiced shooting out in the desert on Sundays, her only day off.

No, the real problem was something she'd read about only today: extra-tight, armed security for Childress's lecture on August tenth. Something about fear that his death or injury could anger the U.S. Congress and seriously damage Mormon self-rule. And Childress had plenty of Mormon enemies.

That meant soldiers packing the lecture hall. When that trapdoor flew open, Lily realized, those rough-and-ready trained killers would have no idea what was afoot. And as all that bright red paint splashed the audience, it would get ugly for her. Perhaps even lethal, once confused soldiers saw "bloody" citizens screaming all around them. This little space in the rafters would become a target.

"So be it," she said softly, but with determination. "Just means you have to be even more precise and efficient."

The bucket of red paint, covered tightly, sat nearby. Lily had already practiced with water and knew how long it would take to fill the paraffin cups, which were firmly melted onto the panel, with paint.

It was time for a dry run.

"I wait until he's well into his talk," she murmured, "and the audience absorbed. Then I drop the trap"—she shot a bolt and the hinged panel sprang open—"and the paint splashes the audience with wider dispersal thanks to all the cups. But I ignore the audience, for I'll have only a few seconds to shoot Childress before he runs for cover."

She aimed her Colt Pocket Model out the opening, centering the muzzle on the speaker's dais. Her finger curled around the trigger, and just then a volley of actual shots erupted somewhere out in town, making her flinch.

Then she realized: it was probably Skye, paying tonight's attackers back in their own coin. Criminals . . . just like she would become next Saturday. A murderer who would probably be hanged or shot—and perhaps Saunders Lee, her favorite among the Mormons, would be in charge of the death squad.

Let it come—her course was set. With luck and steady nerves, she'd make sure the inhumane man who killed her Jimmy would never kill again.

"Sorry, friend," Fargo told the clerk in the gun shop. "I can't accept this."

Fargo set two one-hundred-count boxes of shells onto the deal counter.

A heavyset clerk with nervous eyes frowned at him. "Why not?"

"I expected factory ammo, this is hand-crimped."

"It's all one."

"In a pig's ass," Fargo told him, his manner turning a little harder. "Hand-crimped can't even be reliably tested since each cartridge is different."

The clerk shook his head stubbornly. "Be that as it may, the law says hand-crimped is all I can sell to outlanders."

"Yeah, but I'm here now," Fargo said with a steely eyed smile. "That makes me an *in*lander, right?"

A grin finally cracked the clerk's face. "That makes sense, Brother Fargo. Here's your factory ammo."

The scene, when Fargo emerged onto the street, was not exactly bedlam but it was bizarre for Salt Lake City. It was only midmorning, on the day before the Salt Lake Run, but already there were men in the street drunk as Davy's saw. Everywhere people were cooking deer, elk, and buffalo fish (pulled from Great Salt Lake and named for the hump on its back). Laborers, clerks, farmers, grocers, tailors, doctors, miners, drifters and bag-line bums, even clergy—all starved for a festive holiday.

"Skye!"

Captain Lee, patrolling on his handsome gray, waved at Fargo and reined in.

"What's on the spit, Saunders?" Fargo greeted him.

"That was quite a shooting spree in your room last night, huh?"

"Arrest anybody?" Fargo asked, just for show.

Saunders shook his head. He noticed the ammo boxes in Fargo's hand. "Funny thing . . . you weren't home when a city roundsman was sent to record your story. While you were out, there was another eruption of gunfire, this time over on Poplar Street somewhere."

Fargo feigned innocence under his friend's scrutiny. "Could've been rowdy visitors," he suggested. "Plenty in town."

"Mm . . . well, based on what you've told me, and assuming you're right, that attack on you last night would have been the brainchild of Childress, right?"

Fargo nodded.

Saunders cursed, a rarity for him. "Skye, of course I'd like a shot at that mail contract, it could set me—and a wife and family—up for life. But I'd prefer to see you drop out of this race."

"Drop?— The hell for?"

"Because any man's luck has to play out eventually, even yours. They've been trying to kill you since Mormon Station. You've beat every attempt, including last night, but things'll be different tomorrow. Dangerously different."

"How you figure that?" Fargo asked. He already agreed with Saunders about tomorrow, but he wanted to hear his thinking on the subject.

"Until now you were free to be what you are: a trailsman. You had the luxury of using your excellent eyes and ears, of moving slow and deliberately, of reading sign when you wanted to. But tomorrow you have a grueling race to win. You'll have to hold a breakneck pace with very little time to study your surroundings."

Fargo had to concede the point. It was a bone orchard out in that desert, no, that saline hell. The course wasn't all flat and open, either. There were canyons, dry washes, steep-sided gulches . . . plenty of spots for an ambusher to hide.

"It'll be a rough piece of work," he replied. "But it's time for me and Stover to get huggin', anyhow, so I'm ready."

"What transpires between you two outside city limits," Saunders said, "is a territorial matter. Good luck. I just wish there was some evidence against Childress or McGinnis," Saunders lamented. "Something that might convince my superiors they need to be investigated."

"Something like this?" Fargo asked.

He pulled the folded broadsheet from his pocket and handed it to Saunders, who unfolded it and read an anti-Indian screed under the title "Nits Make Lice!"

"Where'd you get this?" the soldier asked. "It does violate the peace-and-tranquillity laws. But by itself it doesn't prove much. Could've come from anywhere."

"Well, unless McGinnis notices the loose boards in his shed, you'll find an entire box of these on his property. Is that better evidence?"

Saunders nodded, fighting off a smile. "Find them where? Near where those 'rowdy visitors' fired rounds last night?"

"I think so, yep."

Something else seemed to occur to Saunders. "According to the police version of events last night, there was a female with you?"

Instantly Fargo was on guard. He had taken plenty of pains, before he and Lily met last night, to make sure she wasn't Saunders's girl. But mistakes happened in the mental fog of lust.

"Yeah," he replied. "Uhh . . . did the roundsman's report name her?"

Saunders shook his head. "Women aren't named in such . . . lewd incidents."

"Good policy. I'm not the type to mention female names myself."

"And I'm not the type to ask," Saunders assured him, sounding a little curt all of a sudden, to Fargo. "Not that I'll need to. The gossip mill is already churning out supposed facts."

The two men parted, some unspoken tension between them. Fargo hoofed it toward the livery stable at the western end of Commerce Street. Since yesterday the Ovaro had been enjoying the top-of-the-line treatment from Micajah Jones: crushed grain, sweetened water, liniment rubs.

Thinking of the Ovaro, and noticing how isolated the livery was, made Fargo think. His enemies had repeatedly failed to kill the Trailsman. But time was pressing now, and killing his horse would be just as effective.

His premonition proved chillingly sound. Fargo quickened his step, rounded the corner of a large emporium, and spotted thick black clouds of smoke against the china blue sky. A south wind kept them from drifting over town and alerting the residents.

Just then, however, someone did spot the smoke.

"Fire!" a scratchy old voice erupted. "Hell's a-poppin'! The livery's on fire!"

Unfortunately, the livery was the last structure on Commerce Street before it turned into empty desert. Although the fire had been spotted, there was no one near to lend a hand immediately. Fargo soon overtook several other running men, his knees and elbows pumping furiously.

Fargo was first to reach the burning livery, his gut twisted with dread. The blaze must have been set to start fast, and the hay and straw spread everywhere was a natural accelerant. Flames licked up two sides of the barn, and black smoke roiled from the big double doors.

But what truly sickened Fargo were the panicked cries of the horses trapped within. Amid the din, he heard a whinny he recognized, followed by several loud hoof cracks and the sound of splintering wood. Moments later, the Ovaro charged through the smoky doorway, then calmly trotted over to greet his master. The wily stallion, conditioned to survival under desperate circumstances, had kicked the stall door open and saved himself.

Fargo couldn't spot Micajah anywhere outside. Choking in the smoke, dodging licking tongues of fire, he ducked inside and dropped to his knees to see better.

"Jesus!"

He could see horses rearing up, eyes rolling back in baleful fear until the sockets were nearly all white. Micajah had been brained, judging from the blood soaking his tangled nest of hair, then thrown onto a stack of hay bales to hasten his death. The stack was burning at the edges when Fargo grabbed the old hostler, tossed him over his shoulder, and hustled him outside into the hoof-packed yard.

By now other men had shown up, and horses were bolting to safety, even escaping into the desert. Saunders came galloping up and swung out of the saddle. He glanced at the Ovaro, then at Fargo and Micajah, on the ground at Fargo's feet.

"Dead?" the soldier asked.

"Have you et Johnson grass, Captain?" Micajah groused as he sat slowly up, wincing.

"Easy, old salt," Fargo said. "Glad to see you sassy. Did you see whoever hit you?"

"Nope. I'uz pounding caulks into horseshoes, that's the last I recall. 'Cept for a thump like a mule kicking my head. Anyhow, the tack room is separate, the saddles and bridles are safe."

Saunders looked at Fargo. Neither man had to mention any names. But Saunders did. "It's safe to guess, is it, that Dill Stover's roan isn't among those horses now galloping across the desert in a panic?"

"Yeah, but this attempt at the livery wasn't about killing any horse but mine," Fargo said. "Since I got so 'personal' last night, they're striking back in kind."

"And you still want to race tomorrow?"

Fargo glanced at the wounded hostler, then at the barn that would not be saved. Tomorrow he started by squaring off against Dill Stover, and then he was going after the rest.

"Still want to race?" Fargo repeated. "More than ever, my friend, more than ever."

12

"Ladies and gentlemen," the race official bellowed, "the sun has just risen. Despite the disaster yesterday at Micajah Jones's livery, which could have been much worse, the Salt Lake Run will be under way in less than thirty minutes."

Fargo was surprised at the size of the crowd, which now raised a cheer. Despite the early hour, many hundreds of spectators had made the twenty-mile journey to the point, due west of the city, where the road ended and Great Salt Lake Desert began. Some were even taking spots farther along the course. Horse racing was the greatest sport in the West, and the Salt Lake Run the most grueling course yet laid out. Some of these spectators had placed huge wagers on the outcome, and newspaper interest was high.

"There are eleven manned stations along the race course," the official explained, "one every ten miles. Each rider has a number on his saddle, and that number will be recorded when he rides past the station official. No rider can be declared a winner unless he's passed all eleven stations. Thus, we ensure that no one can 'cut' any part of the course, use relay horses, and so forth."

Some of the riders—a field of about thirty had shown up—were only now arriving, many hauling their horses in conveyances to save the mount's vigor. Fargo had simply ridden out the night before and camped, allowing the Ovaro plenty of rest.

"As for the water rules," the official boomed on, "for humanitarian reasons there will be water at each station. *But* . . . requesting water at any station, except number six at the halfway point, means immediate disqualification. So you riders must take some water with you."

This had been Fargo's biggest sticking-point: weight limits. Every single pound would tell, once the desert and the exertion teamed up against the Ovaro. Yet, they had to pack enough water along to keep man and beast alive and reasonably healthy in a merciless climate where a man's urine sometimes evaporated before it hit the ground. Fargo settled on two canteens for himself and a larger gut bag for the Ovaro, who would be doing most of the work.

A chorus of "oohs!" and "aahs!" suddenly burst from the crowd. But Fargo was busy dabbing the Ovaro generously with gall salve at any point where a cinch might rub. As he worked he kept his eyes darting to all sides—it had been a long time since so many people were trying so stubbornly to kill him.

"Don't you at least want to see the balloon, Skye?" a melodic female voice teased him.

He knew it was Dora even before he glanced up and saw her in the pale morning sunshine, pearly teeth flashing at him from between those heart-shaped, kissable lips.

Dora pointed toward the parti-colored balloon just now rising into view to the east, over the city. "It was a sunrise ascension. Pretty, huh?"

Fargo, whose eyes had stayed on her, nodded and said, "Pretty as a royal flush, actually."

"Me or the balloon?"

Fargo grinned. "Balloon? What balloon?"

Dora laughed, then glanced around to make sure she couldn't be heard. "Big talk! I wasn't that good, was I? That night in Mormon Station, I mean. That's how come you haven't been around for more."

"Wasn't that good?" Fargo protested. "Angel, you take second prize to no woman."

Dora looked askance. "Thank you, but that line came out of your pocket like an old coin. And you've pulled it out before."

True enough, but it wasn't Fargo's fault if women were an insecure bunch. He meant what he'd said about Dora.

"Anyhow," she hurried on, "it *will* be good next time, Skye, I promise. I've been thinking about . . . things I'd like to do with you. *To* you."

Fargo looked past Dora's shoulder and felt the dark fear of doomsday. *Oh, hell, here it comes,* he told himself, for just then a mule trolley from Salt Lake City had disgorged its passengers, and Lily Snyder was among them. The last thing Fargo wanted now was a damned catfight, himself separating all the claws.

"The family here, too?" Fargo asked to steer Dora off the steamy and dangerous topics. He turned his back toward the newly arrived Lily before she'd spotted him.

"Everybody's here, we've built a little blanket tent just past the end of the road. John, the kids, even Estelline insisted on coming to cheer you on."

Fargo smiled kindly. "Thanks. But, Dora, you folks won't even see anything, after the start of the race, until the finish."

"I know," Dora said, "but there will be mirrors at every station, relaying back reports. After all you did for us—*and me*—it's impossible not to be here."

Lily, meantime, was glancing around, and Fargo knew she'd soon spot him. Only a damn fool, he reminded himself, ever got trapped in the company of two women he'd topped, especially the most recent two. Killers were already making things lively enough, he figured, and he didn't need the added danger of an "excitable" woman—and Lily, especially, struck him as the type with a hair-trigger temperament.

An unexpected voice startled Fargo. "Don't worry about speed, boy. Won't matter all that much."

Old Micajah Jones, looking a bit pale after yesterday's attack.

"Speed's nothing," Micajah repeated. "Half these horses will collapse before sundown. Hold a lope or a fast trot until the last ten-mile stretch, save his vinegar for the very end. Wash out his nostrils and his mouth every two hours."

Fargo listened close and said nothing. Micajah was more horse than man.

"Sir?" Dora spoke up, realizing the old man must be an expert on horses. "Everybody's arguing about it—is Skye's horse good enough to win against Dill Stover's?"

Micajah cut a corner off his plug with a jackknife, eyes taking in the petite beauty. "Well, miss, Stover's horse has Arabian blood, and will have some advantage in the desert. But there'll be no better horse on the sage today than that pinto stallion," he assured her.

His eyes shifted to Fargo as he added, "Happens the race is honest, Skye'll win in a squeaker. Look here, miss."

Micajah, kneecaps popping, knelt and pointed at Fargo's boots. "Lookit how they're almost worn through on the stirrup side. That's a man at home in the saddle."

Micajah stood up again and stroked the Ovaro's withers, his walnut-wrinkled face wistful. "If youth but knew and age could do . . . this old cob would love a chance at this race. Ain't been many to match it."

As the sun continued to rise and take on more color and heat, Fargo was greeted by others he knew: Saunders Lee, in charge of security; Elder Winslowe, his leg bandaged; Elder West, accompanied by the Emmericks, both of whom were civil to the Trailsman and seemed proud he was in their boardinghouse. Fargo also knew some of the riders. The Far West might be a big place, but, socially speaking, it was still a small world.

And, to prove it, Dill Stover walked past, leading his roan gelding.

"Look," Micajah muttered, "the blamed fool has slit his horse's nostrils."

Fargo did look and spotted dried blood encrusting the roan's nose. Slitting nostrils was an old Indian trick to supposedly increase a horse's wind. It was legal, in most races, but frowned upon.

Stover, perhaps sensing he was being watched, stopped and looked over at Fargo.

"You got a problem, Fargo?" he demanded belligerently.

"Not for much longer," Fargo assured him, adding a nervy little grin. "Today, Junior, is the day of reckoning."

"That's for damn sure, peckerwood."

Stover dropped the reins and walked closer, his eye on Dora. She was a looker, and Stover always liked to dazzle a pretty gal. And he was in a taunting mood.

"Life is a mite queer, Fargo. First you have a close call in your bed, then your horse has one in his stall. You two best not sleep together, huh?"

Fargo, one to rile cool, watched Stover with bored but wary eyes.

"You cowards are all alike," he told Stover. "All the bluff and bluster is to hide your yellow spine."

This struck a nerve, and Stover's response proved Fargo right.

"Know what, Fargo?" he demanded. "I'm half a mind to baste your bacon before the race even starts. Right in front of your pretty little dolly-bird here. Wha'd'ya say to that, big man?"

"I say t'hell with all this chin music," Fargo replied in a bored tone just before he sailed a leather-knuckled haymaker into the side of Stover's blunt jaw.

The blow rocked Stover sideways on his heels. Fargo, a cold and controlled hatred steeling his features, waded in quickly and knocked Stover's head back and forth with a series of fast one-two punches.

Fargo's last blow left Stover doing a slow Virginia reel. Fargo tossed him with a rolling hip lock to get him out of their immediate area. He landed in an ungainly heap beneath his horse.

"I enjoyed that, son," Micajah said. "But it'll be even rougher sledding now."

"Can't get any rougher than it is. Since we can't mend it, we'll end it."

A bugle call summoned all riders to the staging area.

"Good luck, Skye!" Dora called out as he hit leather and swung aboard.

"Good luck?" he repeated, teasing her. "Haven't you looked into your 'peeping stone' to see who wins?"

" 'Fraid to!"

Fargo was wheeling the Ovaro when Lily spotted him and came running over. Fargo pretended not to see her in all the dust and confusion, spurring the stallion quickly forward. But Fate mocked his clever escape: when he glanced back, Dora and Lily stood side by side. With both of them being outlanders and the same sex and age, how long would it take them to start eagerly comparing notes about Skye Fargo?

The contestants drew their mounts abreast in a long line. Some horses will fight the saddle while others save it for the rider, and now it took several minutes for a few riders to gentle their mounts.

Stover, still looking a little punch-drunk, came struggling up last. But he wouldn't struggle, Fargo knew, once that roan of his got the smell of sage in those slit nostrils.

"Ready!" bellowed the official through cupped hands.

Fargo slipped the riding thong over the hammer of his Colt. He glanced left and saw Stover staring at him, blood still trickling from his nose. The man's eyes, two burning pools of acid, promised Fargo a hard death.

"Set!"

Fargo lowered himself in the saddle and shortened the reins.

Bam!

The starter discharged a British dueling pistol into the air, and the long-anticipated Salt Lake Run was under way.

He Bear's wound, suffered at the hands of Skye Fargo during the dawn raid outside Salt Lake City, had not been serious. A bullet had taken the last joint off a finger, and since it was not a trigger finger, he did not care. In his life he had been shot by bullets and arrows, stabbed, lanced, clubbed, and burned over a torture fire. The wound itself was a trifling thing.

But there was a sobering truth: wampum-belt pictographs, and the annual painted histories red men called the winter count, all recorded the same fact. A wound, inflicted by an enemy with powerful medicine, could be used to suck the soul out of a man, and with it his courage.

And He Bear would need all his courage today. So all morning long, while Sister Sun followed her sky-road, he prepared a sweat bath high up on a steep wall of Spanish Canyon.

He made a small hut from hides draped over a frame of branches. Then he stripped naked, even removing the leather wrist band that protected him from the slap of bow strings. When the rocks inside were heated red hot, he poured cold water on them and breathed the hot steam. When he emerged, glistening from the steam, he rubbed his body with sage and plunged into a cool seep spring near the camp.

"Brother," he called over to Nothing but Trouble, who stood nearby on a little sandstone ledge, watching the canyon floor far below, "many things came clear to me in the sweat lodge. By the sun and the earth I live on, I despise this yellow eyes called Childress. Like the pork eater, Stover, he has no honor or true courage. They kill only to profit, never to test their courage against their enemies."

113

"You have caught truth firmly by the tail," Nothing but Trouble agreed. He was busy braiding a huge catch net from horsehair strands. "I would not leave my pony with either man."

Spanish Canyon was a sudden surprise in the midst of Great Salt Desert. A magnificent cataract tumbled down from atop a limestone cliff in an explosion of white foam. There were even swatches of forest on the canyon floor, twenty-foot alder and aspen. To reach this isolated spot they followed a high-country trail so steep even pack mules had been known to fall off.

"Childress," He Bear said, "grew red in his pale face with he told us Fargo *must* be killed here. He even insulted and threatened us."

"As you say. But I have no ears for such words."

Indian leaders did not "dictate" to their people, and He Bear and Nothing but Trouble did not worry overly much about orders from Childress. They did what suited their purposes. They might or might not kill Fargo, but first they had to test such a great man's courage, see if he was the man rumor said he was.

He Bear said, "We should tread carefully here, brother. Childress has much to give in trade goods. We have both seen Indians, even once-proud warriors such as my cousin Swift Canoe, tilling the ground with crude, pointed sticks. We too could become squaw men if we succumb to pride."

He nodded at the catch net taking shape in his friend's hands. "We will kill Fargo and give proof to Childress as he demands. But first we will use pain to discover what manner of man he truly is."

At the crack of the dueling pistol, Fargo disappointed most of the spectators. The rest of the racers, with a few exceptions, loosed great whoops and tore off in a thunder of hooves and a giant white pall of salt dust. Fargo, however, meant to follow Micajah's advice. He simply squeezed the Ovaro with his knees and they set off at a fast trot.

As he advanced, spectators scattered along the first part of the route roweled him.

"Hey, Fargo, bricks tied to your tail?"

"Fargo, kick the brake lever off!"

"Oh, white lightning!"

Fargo met the remarks with good-natured grins and held his pace. Stover had torn off like a scalded dog and had to be well out ahead. Fargo hoped so, anyway, because one of the biggest drawbacks in desert racing were the dust clouds. They were a menace because they disguised a rider's identity until he was well upon you—say, at easy handgun range.

The sun was well up when Fargo passed Station #1 and had his number, twenty-four, recorded. The mirror signalman excitedly flashed news of the Trailsman's arrival. Surprisingly, two sheepish looking riders milled about the station, having already dropped out of the race. Their horses had nearly collapsed from that hard, flashy start.

By midmorning great white sails of cloud flowed across a sky of bottomless blue. The ruthless sun had weight as well as warmth as it lay on Fargo's shoulders and the back of his neck.

The next ten miles showed two more victims of poor judgment. One was leg-trapped under his dead sorrel, and Fargo paused long enough to throw off and pull him loose. The other had shot his horse when it started convulsing and blowing bloody foam.

"That's four down and twenty-six to go, Skye!" shouted a voice behind him.

He looked over his shoulder. Because the rider's horse was only trotting, like the Ovaro, the dust cloud wasn't so thick. Fargo recognized a carrot-topped Welshman named Jay Hobert. The two men had once teamed up to freight cookstoves into the Sierra gold towns.

"Still riding the coyote dun, I see," Fargo greeted him when the two men rode side by side.

He looked askance at the knock-kneed, stave-ribbed gelding. It was of good disposition, he recalled, but getting long in the tooth.

"I know, I know," Hobert said, reading his face, "me and Fire-away here ain't got a snowball's chance of taking the laurels today. I'm just curious to see can he finish? Plenty today won't, you know."

Fargo nodded, Jay's remark coming just as Fargo became aware that a white cloud was boiling toward him from ahead—as if a rider had deliberately wheeled around to come at him.

Stover attacking? Fargo knocked loose the Colt's riding thong even as he tugged left rein to drift wide.

The boiling white cloud shifted with him.

"God's trousers!" Jay Hobert exclaimed, for the mystery rider was now hurtling toward them like a cannonball. "Jesus Christ, look out, Skye!"

Hobert, who'd been caught flat-footed, went for his single-shot pistol. But just as he raised it to fire into the whirling dervish, his spooked horse crow-hopped sideways, and the bullet shot nothing but empty sky.

Fargo couldn't yet bring himself to plug an unseen target, nor was there time for that anyway. He waited until the approaching salt-dust cloud was within spitting distance, then tugged rein hard right.

The Ovaro responded with the skill and timing of a show horse. The rider thundered past, but Fargo was so close now he saw there *wasn't* any rider, just a wild-eyed buckskin and an empty saddle. Fargo hoped the downed rider wasn't still lying on the desert floor.

"That's at least five down," Jay said cheerfully. "None of 'em ever bought *us* a beer."

Fargo grinned at the gallows humor, though there was no way to pretend he himself might get lucky. It wasn't just Dill Stover he'd have to settle accounts with. Those two Utes were out there somewhere, too, ready to pile on the agony. And the race itself was already brutal enough.

"I wish I *could* win this damn race," Jay said wistfully. "Besides a sweet little pot, a mail contract. Oh, mama! No more hog and hominy on *my* plate."

The mail contract . . . that got Fargo thinking about Saunders again and this mysterious gentile female of his. Lily said nothing about any suitor, but Saunders acted a little testy when he brought up the identity of the woman with whom Fargo was caught. As for Lily—Fargo had no proof, but she was up to something. A redhead "drenched in blood" . . . something tragic on August tenth . . . Childress speaking on that day. . . .

"Holy shit," Fargo said aloud. "Childress and Jimmy, her husband who 'died.' Died of overpriced water, likely."

"You going simple in this heat?" Jay teased.

"Sorry, just tying up loose threads."

That crazy little hothead, Fargo now realized, had got some damn fool notion of killing Childress to avenge her husband. There could be no other logical reason for her to stay in Salt Lake City, a place she disliked. A woman with her looks could make a good life for herself anywhere— but the lust for revenge would also *keep* a person anywhere. Without question that monster Childress needed killing. But these Mormons would almost surely execute her, for their murder laws did not make sex distinctions.

Now and then vast sage slopes rose to right or left. Fargo read the time in the slant of the sun. As he had every two hours, he reined in and swung down. He flung the bridle and washed out the Ovaro's nostrils and mouth with a wet bandanna. Then he gave the stallion two hatfuls of water and drank a few swallows from his canteen.

Man and horse wanted more water than this. But it was enough to keep them alive and forging on.

"Fargo's still a poor showing!"

Cecil McGinnis, his face flush with triumph, returned to the silver-spruce-lined side yard of his house on Poplar Street. Out front on the street a newsboy was walking up and down, calling out the latest mirror-flash reports.

"That's three stations reporting now, and Fargo is among the drag riders eating everybody else's dust," McGinnis reported as he joined Childress again. "Perhaps we overrated him, and that contract is ours after all."

Childress, his linen immaculate and every hair in place, pointed his chin toward the damaged house.

"Destroyed the glass, the frame, and the casing. Even managed to nick your elbow with a shard of glass. A very gutsy showing after what he went through in his room. The man's nerve is so cool he pisses icicles. We haven't overrated him, Cecil."

McGinnis lost some of his triumphant flush. "You don't believe Stover could beat him—without help, I mean?"

"Let's just say . . . even a bad dog is worth a bone. If Dill does pull this off today, one way or another—then he'll not only keep the two hundred fifty dollar prize, I'll add two hundred fifty dollars more."

McGinnis grinned at the sincere tone in his partner's

voice. "Once the stupid oaf realizes the value of the contract he has already signed away, he's going to howl bloody murder."

"Yes," Childress said quietly, "bloody murder—that's exactly right. Because he knows too damn much and he has a big mouth. After today he's useless to us. Was before today, actually."

"The Utes?"

Childress nodded, gazing around the rest of the yard and trying to guess what else might have interested Fargo last night.

"The Utes, yes indeed," he said. "Oh, they've definitely disappointed us this past week. They've done better work for us in the past, but lately they're sandbagging. Frankly, I suspect they admire Fargo and would rather kill Stover."

"Red men of insight, eh? Well, they'll get their chance."

Childress nodded, eyes narrowing as he looked at the shed out back. "Anything incriminating back there?"

"I doubt it," McGinnis said. "If there is, it's a fart in a blizzard compared to what's up in Mormon Station."

"Speaking of that—Saunders Lee has had his eye on us for some time," Childress said, thinking out loud. "And I've seen him huddling with Fargo. We may have to move some things."

"Not so long as you're Brigham's favorite," McGinnis reminded him. "My God, you're guest speaker at the Civic Lecture Hall next Saturday. Even I haven't been invited."

Childress compressed his thin lips in a straight frown. "Favor and fortunes turn quickly out here, you know that. Especially with a volatile substance like Fargo in the mix. That bastard is implacable. If he survives today, we had better come up with a good plan fast. Because he means to sink us, Cecil. Sink us six feet closer to hell."

13

The afternoon heated up to an oven fierceness as the searing white sun westered. Skye Fargo's hair was often sweat-soaked, but when he took his hat off, his scalp dried in mere moments. The hot, dry air was so thirsty for moisture it sucked up every droplet almost instantly.

Fargo kept a palm on his Colt at all times now, for the terrain was not always open desert, and there were numerous ambush points. He feared the Utes more than he feared Stover, but it was almost pointless to watch for them. He already knew they would never dismount and take up positions, white-man style, among the rocks and bushes. Indians seldom forted up, just as they followed little group discipline in a battle, relying on individual courage and initiative to inspire others at key moments.

Because he had conserved the Ovaro's stamina for so long by trotting him, Fargo now had the option of holding a lope, occasionally even a brief run when the Ovaro pulled against the reins. Jay Hobert was well behind him now, out of sight. Fargo was an old friend of solitude, but he missed the conversation.

"How we doing?" Fargo inquired as he finally reined in at Station #6 and swung down a little stiffly. He threw the bridle so the Ovaro could drink from a wooden tank.

"Lots better than you were doing, Mr. Fargo," a bearded, burly Mormon informed him. "Dill Stover was well out in front, but you're closing the lead. His horse looks strong yet, but I'd guess it hasn't been as well-paced as yours. A horse like that, sure it's fast. But that roan is not a bright horse, it's the kind stupid enough to run itself to death. And, no offense to your people, Dill Stover is mean enough to let it."

"He ain't my people, either, friend. Who's running third?"

"Hard to say, but nobody's even close."

Fargo stretched the small of his back. Like his saddle-ravaged tailbone, it felt like somebody had been hammering on it for hours. Then he took his hat off and plunged his head into the tank. The water wasn't even remotely cool, but at least it was wet.

He refilled his canteens from casks on the back of a wagon. When he drank, Fargo had to use the first three mouthfuls just to rinse the salt dust out of his mouth. Then, while the Ovaro finished drinking, Fargo quickly stripped the tack down to the neck leather and draped the sweat-soaked saddle blanket over the sideboards of the wagon to dry in the fierce heat. He quickly wiped the stallion off with a feed sack.

"No wonder you're showing strong," the station official approved, watching Fargo. "You're the first rider today I've seen take that much trouble with his horse."

"How many riders out for good, you figure?"

"At least ten, I b'lieve, as of last report. Prob'ly more like a dozen by now."

Fargo nodded. He had spotted several more himself. Two standing over dead or dying mounts, another leading a lame horse. Micajah had predicted that half of today's riders would come a cropper. Looked like he was about right.

But as Fargo reset the Ovaro's saddle, he reminded himself—now that the distance was narrowing between him and Stover, the attack could come at any moment.

The terrain itself, after station #6, favored an ambush. For perhaps twenty minutes he rode through a precipice-walled canyon before emerging out onto the salt plain again. Fargo kept his Henry to hand, but he saw nothing more dangerous than a snake curled atop a hot rock.

An hour later the race course dipped into a narrow bottom. Even out here, in the ghastly heart of the *borrasca* wasteland, new life was budding. Fargo could hear the melodious, if unlikely, singing of meadowlarks. But he ignored the fragile beauty of the desert and remained alert for the trouble he knew was coming.

A stream of alkalai water meandered through the bottom. Fargo crossed it on a shallow gravel ford. The Ovaro whinnied nervously at the sound of hot springs rumbling just beneath the surface.

Fargo cleared the bottom and headed out onto the baking flats again. Huge Spanish Canyon was coming up soon, and Fargo considered it the most dangerous stretch of the course. He had scouted through it, several years ago, and found plenty of signs of various Indian tribes.

Despite Fargo's vigilance, he didn't expect trouble before Spanish Canyon. Thus he was caught completely by surprise when a rider suddenly dashed out of a concealed ravine to Fargo's right.

At first, thanks to the roiling billows of white dust, Fargo could see neither horse nor rider. But the pounding sound was definitely that of iron-shod hoofs. Fargo was riding along a clay-baked ridge, and the dust cleared as soon as his attacker reached the hardpack.

Dill Stover, both hands in view to show he wasn't employing firearms. "Keep it clean, Fargo! This is just a little sport!"

"Yellow-bellied bastard," Fargo muttered.

Stover could have filled his hand before charging and settled this like a man. But, while willing to kill a man from a distance or in the back, he wouldn't take the risk of facing him fair and square. He was counting on Fargo not to shoot, but the Trailsman drew his Colt anyway, unsure how this would play out.

Now he saw Stover's magnificent roan at its best as it charged strong and fast, great divots of earth flying up behind it. Stover was showing off, playing the trick rider to dazzle Fargo—swinging from one side of his horse to another and running along the ground while holding the saddle horn.

"Real pretty!" Fargo roared out as Dill and the roan rushed closer like a ramming ship. "But the Sioux and the Cheyenne are better."

"Better than *this*, peckerwood?" Stover yelled back, and moments later he viciously quirted the Ovaro across the nose as they flashed past at a gallop, missing Fargo and the Ovaro by a few inches.

The stallion, enraged, almost gave chase, but Fargo tightened the reins. It might have been a cliché from nickel novels, but Fargo felt his trigger finger literally itching to shoot Stover.

"Easy, old warhorse, easy," Fargo soothed. "The cat sits by the gopher hole and bides his time. Here they come again."

Stover had wheeled the roan and they were thundering back toward Fargo and his horse. Fargo heard the slicing *whacks* as Stover rapidly quirted his roan from side to side.

"That gelding, stupid or not, is holding up like a champion," Fargo marveled. "But it's only a horse and this country out here is hell's badlands. That stupid son of a bitch Stover will run him into the ground before this day is over. Easy, boy, stand easy," he added as his pinto began sidestepping.

Fargo couldn't blame the Ovaro. Standing still, while another horse charged, went against all its instincts. Fargo could have taken evasive action to avoid, then lose, Stover. But the effort required to do so was more trouble and risk, in this country, than tolerating Stover and seeing where this was headed.

"That stallion's a spavined nag, Fargo!" Stover taunted just before he again quirted the Ovaro hard. This time Fargo had to use the bit hard to hold the stallion in place.

Anger steeled his features, and it took all Fargo's discipline not to start burning powder, beginning with that roan.

"Third time's the charm," he assured his horse while Stover, still laughing, doubled back for some more fun. "And if it's not, I *will* shoot the bastard and do the world a favor."

Fargo realized how confident Stover must feel if he could afford to lose time playing these little spite games when there was a race to win.

"Easy goes it," Fargo soothed the prancing Ovaro as Stover's roan again bore down on them like a stampede. "Maybe I'll just plug the bastard now, huh?"

Instead, he shortened the reins and kicked both feet out of the stirrup, getting ready. "*This* time the worm will turn."

"Here's one for you, Fargo, *big man*!" Stover's bullhorn voice boomed out.

Fargo waited until the last possible moment, then jerked

back hard on both reins while also thumping his heels hard into the Ovaro's ribs. The powerfully muscled stallion rose straight up on his rear legs and chinned the moon.

Dill Stover had been balanced in one stirrup, most of his body braced to give Fargo a powerful blow. But when Fargo went straight up, Stover's mighty blow with the quirt caught nothing but air. He lost his balance and then his hold, crashing down hard onto the hardpack at a full gallop. Stover began tumbling along like a Russian thistle, howling with pain before he blacked out.

Fargo howled too—with mirth. Even the Ovaro seemed to enjoy the spectacle and gave a whinny of approval. Fargo didn't bother checking on the inert form of Stover, but he hoped like hell the human pond scum was dead or dying. Nor did Fargo worry about the roan, now standing about a quarter-mile off.

"Stover can mind his own halter. We got a race to win," Fargo said as he chucked the Ovaro up to a lope.

Spanish Canyon opened out ahead, entered by a gradually narrowing trail that threaded its way downward through a massive tumble of rocks and boulders. Just as Fargo entered the trail, in an example of one of the desert's strange surprises, thunder suddenly crackled and a brief rain sizzled on the surrounding rocks. All this without a cloud in view and the sun blazing.

A quail, startled by something besides Fargo, darted across his path. The Ovaro caught a scent and lifted his head, trying to turn around. Fargo slewed around in his saddle, then felt a cold hand squeeze his heart. A Ute warrior stood about thirty feet behind him. He slashed one hand through the air, a signal of some sort to a hidden comrade.

Before Fargo could react, a heavy catch net fell around him and was expertly drawn tight, trapping his arms. Too late Fargo realized: Dill Stover's little attack, just before this, was only a diversion. A means of lowering his expectation of a second attack so soon after—and it worked.

The Ovaro reared up, but Fargo was helpless. Somebody tugged hard on the tangled net, and he hit the ground with a bounce.

"Hair Face! I will not eat your *famous* horse!" one of the braves taunted him in English. "It will go on my string. Just as your scrotum will make my next bullet pouch."

Fargo, tangled up in a ball on the ground, could hear the two braves approaching over the rocks. He calmed the Ovaro, fearing it might bolt. These braves might kill his fleeing horse rather than lose whatever Fargo carried.

"So . . . *this* is the great white man the Navajos call Son of Light?"

The voice was right overhead now. Fargo peered out from the tangled strands of the net and glimpsed the same two Utes who had been plaguing him since Mormon Station.

"Son of Light? *I* call him Light of Brains," said the larger of the two. "Because he is stupid he will spend perhaps the next two days suffering the most terrible tortures. And then, when he has no more screams left in him, we will cut off his face and take it to Childress."

"Yes," Fargo said, "you will run to Childress just like obedient white man's dogs. You *talk* like Ute braves, but white men run you."

A startled silence greeted this unexpected insult. For some tribes, Fargo had learned over the years, torture of prisoners was a form of group entertainment. But for the Utes it took on a religious and moral significance. It tested an enemy, measured his worth, proved whether or not the claims about his courage had substance behind them or only wind. Fargo knew the worst thing he could do right now was beg or be meek.

"This thing you just said, Hair Face," the largest Ute assured him, "will cost you the worst hurt in the world."

The point of an obsidian knife blade penetrated the netting and dinted Fargo's throat. Then it pressed harder, like a nail penetrating his windpipe, and he felt warm blood tickling his chest as it streamed down into his shirt. Any harder, Fargo feared, and his vocal cords would be severed.

All this was to hold Fargo motionless while the other brave, a slightly smaller one with a wounded hand, cut away some of the net. He took Fargo's Colt, but because of the way the Trailsman was lying, the brave failed to discover the Arkansas Toothpick in Fargo's boot. They ig-

124

nored the Ovaro for now, seeing he would not flee without his master.

"Here, brave and famous man," said the brave with the slightly wounded hand. "You are nothing without your gun, so here it is."

He cocked the Colt and centered the muzzle on Fargo's forehead right between the eyes. Fargo's heart leaped into his throat. But knowing that showing fear would sink him fast, Fargo kept a poker face as the Ute slowly took up the trigger slack until it was tight. Now, if he pulled it back the width of a cat hair, Fargo knew his brains would be all over the rocks behind him.

At the last possible moment, the Ute laid the revolver tight against the side of Fargo's skull and fired it.

The bullet flew off harmlessly and wasn't Fargo's problem—his trouble was the detonation itself. He couldn't help a hard, fast twitch as an explosive pain and a shattering din left his skull and ears ringing. The Indians shouted taunts, but he heard nothing and feared he was permanently deaf. Slowly, however, his hearing returned like feeling to a limb that had fallen asleep.

"I've noticed something," Fargo managed. "You two always stay close to each other. As lovers will."

Such an insult, to most Indian braves, was suicidal in its recklessness. And Fargo very nearly died on the spot when the bigger one started toward him, face bloating with rage and knife in hand. But he settled for kicking Fargo several good ones to the ribs and head.

"You pretend this loud show of strength," he told Fargo. "Let us see if you can quietly pass the test of manhood."

While the smaller brave covered Fargo with a Colt revolving rifle, the other gathered fist-sized rocks. Using matches taken from Fargo, he made a fire and heated up several of the rocks. Fargo's shirt was pulled off and he was staked out spread-eagle.

Fargo knew what was coming, and he tasted the coppery bile of fear and dread. But there was no option now but to stick with his strategy of taunting and insulting.

"You two lovers seem excited now," he mocked, ribs aching from all the kicks. "Which one plays the bull and which the cow?"

Just then, watching them glower at him, Fargo finally realized something—it was the furrows between an Indian's eyes that made him look so menacing when he frowned, as these two did now.

"He has a brave mouth," the bigger warrior said as he turned away from the fire. "Let us see if his 'courage' is only lip deep."

The big Ute held a glowing rock between two green sticks. Fargo knew he was in a world of pain now, but no matter how rough it got he dare not scream too much or beg at all.

"Here, Hair Face," the Ute said with a mocking grin. "Tell us: does this feel like the bull or the cow?"

He plopped the hot rock right onto Fargo's bare stomach, and there was an audible crackle of cooking flesh. Pain exploded, turning the entire world bright red. The searing heat made him reflexively try to sit up. Pain that couldn't be measured by any scale tore through him, and Fargo couldn't help a sharp grunt before biting his lip until it bled. At least the rock had rolled off him for now.

"Look, He Bear," the wounded Ute said. "The brave and famous man is about to cry."

But, in truth, Fargo could tell they were both surprised at his lack of reaction. Fargo had been tortured before, and like many men who have undergone such pain, he had developed tricks to help him survive the ordeal. One such trick was to visualize the pain as a red ball in his mind. Then he could imagine himself putting the pain inside a box to contain its spread. It was no magic cure-all, but it helped him.

He put the pain away now and sent a mocking grin up at the smaller Ute.

"Cry?" he repeated. "Little girls, I was only going to ask for more. A puling child could survive this."

Some might think it dangerous and stupid to *ask* for more torture and even insult the torturers. But Fargo's strategy was starting to work—both braves exchanged startled glances at his unexpected response. Respect glimmered briefly in their eyes.

Nonetheless, they were determined to test him further, and Fargo was determined to get back into this race before he lost too much time. He waited until they untied him,

126

planning to bury him up to his neck and set red ants loose on him.

The big Ute, whom the other called He Bear, began scooping out a pit with a coffee can while the second Indian, holding his knife to Fargo's throat, untied his limbs. Fargo waited until both hands were free, then made his move.

Pain exploding in his burned abdomen, he sat up with lightning speed and jerked the Arkansas Toothpick from his boot with his left hand. With his right he slugged the Ute hard, then pulled him to the ground.

By the time He Bear turned around at the commotion, Fargo had his partner in a death hold, knife to his throat. He Bear snatched up his rifle.

"Do it," Fargo warned him, using the Ute's body as a shield, "and you kill your own friend. If your bullet does not strike his lights, my knife will."

"Kill him, He Bear," the brave called out. "I do not value my life at a gnat's breath."

"That doesn't matter," Fargo reminded He Bear, knowing their tribal beliefs. "You know what happens to any Ute who kills a fellow Ute. He will spend all eternity in the Forest of Tears, unclean and outcast."

"We are renegades," He Bear boasted. "These old legends mean nothing to us."

Nonetheless, He Bear's smug, all-powerful manner had undergone a sea change. The Hair Face was right: the killing of a fellow Ute, even by accident, was the greatest sin in the universe. Besides . . . both Utes had lost their pleasure in torturing Fargo when he responded with such manly courage.

"You know, brother," he finally said to Nothing but Trouble, "it is not *this* one who deserves killing."

Here was a crack in their resolve. But Fargo knew he had to help the Indians save face. If they simply let him go, he had defeated them. But Fargo knew the Utes were well familiar with the concept of trading one captive for another. There was no loss of face in such a transaction.

"I propose a trade," Fargo suggested to He Bear. "Your friend's life for mine. That way no man wins or loses."

Finally He Bear nodded and lay his rifle down. The American Indian despised nothing more than a liar, and

Fargo didn't worry about tricks once they agreed to terms. Within a few minutes he was again pounding the saddle, wincing at the pain. He stopped only to cut open a cactus and smear the milky nectar on his burn.

This time he let the Ovaro out to a run. Despite his wounds and burns, despite the fiery pain in his midsection, he *must* try to make up for lost time. This was the stretch where he would be pitted against Stover, and Fargo planned to beat him soundly—and then *beat* him soundly.

14

"You there . . . Captain John-a-dreams."

Saunders Lee was busy keeping an eye on the spectators milling around the finish line, making sure none of them was there to "influence" the end of the race. He glanced up quickly at the sound of a pleasant female voice.

"Why, hello, Lily," he greeted the pretty redhead. "The big race drew you out, too, eh?"

"Esther gave everyone at the boardinghouse, even me, a holiday for the race," she replied, "except poor Louise, the cook."

Despite the encroaching darkness, most of the spectators had stayed around to see the first rider cross the finish line. It didn't matter what hour the riders returned—huge bonfires had been set along the final approach. The entire area was lit up like a parlor at Christmas, and nearly as festive. A band played popular tunes of the day, and a beer tent had been erected.

"The newspapers say that somebody's been trying to kill Skye Fargo since he arrived in Utah Territory," Lily said. "Is that true?"

Saunders gazed at her, trying to read her face. She sent him a bright smile to distract him—that usually worked with men.

"So you know Skye?" Saunders asked her.

Lily was glad it was dark so he couldn't see her blush. "Well, of course, I've met him in the boardinghouse."

"Well, as to the business with someone trying to kill him—I know it's true because Skye told me, not the newspapers," Saunders replied. "And believe me, it's not an unusual situation for him."

129

"Speaking of the newspapers, I've read that security next Saturday, when Frederic Childress speaks at Civic Lecture Hall, will be unprecedented," Lily remarked casually. "Isn't that unusual?"

This time Saunders's eyes narrowed as he studied Lily. "For an outlander, you mean? Yes, but Childress is a tough case. Some Mormons are convinced his pro-Indian speeches and editorials are weakening our hand in defending ourselves. Others dislike him because he's a gentile who's found favor with Brigham Young."

"What do you think of him?" Lily asked bluntly.

"Doesn't matter," Saunders replied diplomatically. "I'm not supposed to think, just follow orders."

"So armed soldiers will be in the lecture hall?"

Again Saunders sent her a speculative look. But Lily was the picture of innocence.

"Yes, lining both side walls. And I'll be in charge."

"My goodness," she said. "I'd hate to be anyone trying to hurt Childress."

"So would I," Saunders said, watching her closely. "The shoot-to-kill orders have come down from above me. At the first sign of trouble, we'll open fire."

Skye Fargo never carried a watch, but he had a good idea, as the twilight gradually thickened, what time it was.

He and the Ovaro made good time now as the terrain once again flattened out. They passed stations seven, eight, and nine, overtaking more riders. Fargo's biggest problem, at the moment, was pain. He had cut open the pod of a cactus and smeared the sticky milk over his burned stomach, soothing it. But he could do nothing to alleviate the painful throbbing where he'd been repeatedly kicked in his head and ribs.

Moonlight riding was easier in salt deserts, where the white sand reflected more light. Which meant rustlers were often afoot after dark, using the desert as a road to drive cattle, stolen from the Mormons, to grasslands northeast of here. Fargo abruptly reined in as he spotted masked and hooded riders out ahead, moving a small herd across the trail.

"None of our picnic, boy," Fargo told his stallion as they waited behind a clutch of boulders. "I just hope they get a wiggle on—we're burning good moonlight."

Fargo didn't enjoy this hiding while he witnessed criminals at work. But he wasn't a badge-toter and saw no reason to butt into every crime he noticed. Besides, he had a race to win.

As he waited, he couldn't help wondering about Stover. He hadn't seen the loutish braggart since Stover went crashing ass-over-applecart off his roan. The problem was, thanks to the little torture session in Spanish Canyon, Fargo had been delayed and had no idea if the man was behind or ahead of him—or even in the race.

The last, straggling steers were crossing the trail ahead, a rustler hazing them. Fargo had made the mistake of not moving far enough downwind—a rustler's horse caught the Ovaro's scent and whinnied.

The boulders were sparse cover and there was no other place to hide well. One of the rustlers raised a shout, spotting him, and the night erupted in gunfire.

A bullet grazed Fargo's left ear in a hot wire of pain. The next thing Fargo knew, three or four rustlers were rushing him, guns blazing.

Long years of experience in tough scrapes helped Fargo make instant decisions. Fleeing was an option since the Ovaro still had good bottom and rustlers would be unlikely to leave their herd long. But the delay could be costly. Better, Fargo decided as he sprang down from the saddle, to do the unexpected and resist. These men were moving stolen beef and hardly had time for a gun battle.

But there was no place to cover down and the rustlers were closing fast, bullets fanning the air all around Fargo. He resorted to a trick he and the Ovaro had used before when caught out in the open plains by a superior force. He threw an arm around the Ovaro's neck and, speaking softly, tugged him down until he was lying flat on one side. Not only did Fargo now have a breastwork, the Ovaro was a much smaller target.

Fargo opened up with the Henry, and immediately the attackers swerved off to join the receding herd.

"Just wasted more time, boy," Fargo complained as he booted his Henry and stepped up into leather. "From here on, old warhorse, it's root hog or die."

The Ovaro understood the urgency of his voice if not the words. He threw back his head and nickered, then sprang into motion like a startled antelope. Fargo let him run now, still saving the gallop, and the stallion seemed to glide across the luminous white surface of the desert.

Station #10 was well behind Fargo, and soon he reached station #11, the last one before the finish in ten miles.

Fargo swung down just long enough to water the Ovaro from his hat.

"How many ahead of me?" he called to the official.

"Only one, Mr. Fargo. Dill Stover."

Fargo felt disappointment and anger thrumming in his blood. "Should've done for that son of a bitch earlier," he muttered as the Ovaro drank.

He turned to the official again. "How far ahead?" he asked.

"Just came through, you can still see his dust haze in the moonlight. But he ain't your only problem—there's a couple riders right behind you, hell-bent for leather."

Fargo, too, had detected the faint vibrations of rapidly approaching hoofs. Things had changed since the report earlier at Station #6, when no one was a close third to him and Stover.

Dill Stover . . . Fargo was damned sick and tired of him.

He clapped his soaking-wet hat on his head, vaulted into the saddle, and finally opened his stallion out to a gallop.

Man and horse were one with the night now, the quick rataplan of hoofs the only sound. Fargo couldn't see him yet, but Stover was only a fox-step away—his dust trail was thicker now, and Fargo pulled his bandanna over his mouth and nose.

The Ovaro, who hadn't been pushed for real speed in weeks, had vast stores of it now and didn't need coaxing from Fargo to tap those stores. At moments, as the stallion lengthened his stride, Fargo could have sworn they were literally flying through the desert night.

"There!" Fargo shouted when, through the haze and darkness, a horse and rider were momentarily silhouetted against a white wafer of full moon.

But Fargo had spotted something else, too, something that made his stomach go queasy. Out ahead of Stover was a lighted area that could only be the finish line of the race.

And there wasn't much time to catch and overtake Stover before he'd reach it.

"Hiii-*ya!*" Fargo shouted, lowering himself over the stallion's neck and speaking steadily to him.

A real, honest-to-God horse race had begun now, Fargo versus Stover, the only match the crowd had really cared about. The racers were close enough to the finish now that spectators lined the way.

The lighted area was growing closer, and Fargo could make out the crowd. But the Ovaro was gaining ground on Stover's roan. Fargo realized the wetness spattering his face was Stover's mount, blowing foam.

A triumphant laugh rose above the sound of pounding hoofs.

"Rot in hell, Fargo!" Stover's voice floated back to him. "And after I publicly shame your ass, I'm *still* going to kill you, you peckerwood bastard!"

Fargo ignored the hot-jawing, aware only of the distance to the finish line and Stover's dwindling lead. As the Ovaro's head drew even with the roan's tail, Fargo took the precaution of filling his hand. He knew Stover too damn well.

Stover, glancing over his shoulder, saw the Colt and may have thought it unwise to shoot in front of so many witnesses. But there was still enough darkness to get away with throwing rocks—a supply of which he had in his saddlebag. He suddenly turned in the saddle to hurl one.

It flew low and hit the sole of Fargo's boot. Even so it hurt like hell.

A second rock flew past, and Fargo jerked his head aside just in time.

"Turnabout is fair play, you cowardly son of a bitch!" Fargo shouted.

Being behind, he had a better target than did Stover. Fargo plunged his right hand into a saddlebag and found the extra horseshoe he always carried. He hurled it and had the satisfaction of hearing Stover grunt in surprise and pain.

For a few seconds Stover swayed in the saddle on the brink of falling out. Then he lowered himself over the horn, and the final stretch was on.

Fargo glimpsed faces flash by like fish under water: Saunders Lee, John Beckmann, even Estelline and the oldest kids, all cheering him on. Spectators cheered on both sides of him, and the din was even louder at the finish line itself. The Ovaro, holding strong, not even blowing foam, was about ten feet to the left of the roan and still gaining—his head was now even with Dill Stover, who suddenly looked worried.

"Too late, Fargo!" he bellowed with desperate bravado. "You're too damn late! Watch this and weep, big man!"

Stover began viciously quirting his horse, and gouging it deep in the shoulders with his cruel, star-roweled spurs. As Fargo drew even, however, he noticed the roan wasn't just blowing foam, but bloody foam. The gelding looked desperate, wild-eyed, and its breathing was raspy like a file. That damn fool Stover had pushed it mercilessly.

And still was. The two horses were neck and neck, the two riders hunched low in the saddle, the crowd deliriously cheering. Fargo felt the Ovaro seem to uncoil like a spring, surging past the roan gelding.

Stover cursed like a wild man and spurred his horse even deeper. Fargo and the Ovaro broke through the ribbon to a stupendous roar from the crowd.

"The winner!" an official roared. "Skye Fargo!"

The words were as welcome, to Fargo's ears, as rain to dry earth. They meant the Salt Lake Run was finally over.

A congratulatory throng surrounded his horse. Hands picked him out of the saddle, hoisted him on shoulders, marched him around. Admirers volleyed so many questions at him Fargo couldn't even try to answer them.

The familiar face of Saunders Lee emerged out of the melee. He had noticed Fargo favoring his midsection.

"You all right, Skye?" he shouted close to Fargo's ear. "There's a doc on hand."

"Ah, I'm tolerable well, Saunders. My ass is sore and I've got some burns to grease."

Fargo was actually grateful for the wild crowd of men— they kept Dora and Lily from getting to him right away. Those two had been standing side by side when Fargo left this morning, and by now they probably knew he had bedded both of them. He'd rather return to those Utes in Spanish Canyon than face two pissed-off females.

Riding in, Fargo had noticed something else interesting—

Saunders Lee and Lily talking together and looking mighty cozy. *Jesus,* he wondered again, *did I top my good friend's sweetheart?*

A third rider, soon after a fourth, crossed the line, receiving much less fanfare. Just then, Stover's bullhorn voice bellowed with impressive force, silencing all other noise. "Fargo, God *damn* you!"

Fargo glanced straight ahead. Dill Stover's roan, bloody from vicious spurring, was gasping for breath and staggering. It went to its front knees, whinnied piteously, then simply fell over dead. The final breath, of this once magnificent horse, was long and ghastly as the big lungs emptied of all air.

Stover's rage was ugly to behold in the flickering light of bonfires. He walked slowly in Fargo's direction, breathing so hard his nostrils whistled.

"Want the army to stop him?" Saunders asked Fargo.

Fargo shook his head. "That just leaves the weed to sprout back up. It's past time to rip it out for good."

Fargo's well-wishers had already lowered him to the ground. He had taken his gun belt off so no one would get hurt in the press of the crowd. He buckled it back on as Stover stalked closer, so frustrated and mad he was pounding his fist on his own chest.

"That's right," he told Fargo, "strap on that iron, big man. Goddamn you, Fargo, you've seen your last sunrise!"

Saunders cleared the crowd back as Stover stalked closer, chest heaving with rage.

"I'm just curious," Fargo replied. "You've tried a half-dozen or so times now to kill me from ambush. You really think you're going to do better face to face? I don't. Damn, Dill, think about it—these are your last moments on earth."

Stover had never had the courage to challenge Fargo to a fair fight, and as his first flush of rage passed he began to regret his rash challenge. But he had already made that challenge in front of hundreds of witnesses, and he could hardly swallow back the words now.

Fargo stood hip-cocked, palms resting along his thighs. "C'mon, Dill, what's the holdup? Clear leather so I can end your mother's shame."

Sweat poured down Stover's big, bluff face. "All right, but I got something to say first."

"Then hawk it up," Fargo said, suspecting a fox play.

Stover's hands moved slowly out in front of him, as if simply gesturing while he spoke. "All right, it's just this—"

Quick as a darting lizard, while he was still speaking Stover drew his Smith & Wesson. As Fargo knew he would, the cowardly murderer had to try a trick to distract him. But Fargo's Colt leaped out a fractional second sooner, and he plugged Stover dead center.

The man's knees came unhinged and he fell in a heap, flopping in the sand like a neck-wrung chicken. Fargo had learned to be wary of possum players, so he tossed a finishing shot into the downed man's head.

"That's for Orrin Lofley," he said softly as he leathered his Colt. "He died in my place. Now the ledger's balanced."

Fargo rarely took pleasure in killing. But as he stared at Stover's body, he felt he had truly done the West a favor. The man had been a back-shooting murderer and thief, a poisoner of water holes, and he deserved the hottest room in hell.

The gunfight had mesmerized the crowd, and Fargo turned quietly away, hoping to slip off a few miles and make a camp.

However, the moment he turned away, there was a resounding slap on his left cheek, followed by a powerful swat to the right cheek.

"Skye Fargo, you ought to be horsewhipped!" brunette Dora fumed.

"And then gelded!" redheaded Lily added, eyes blazing.

Fortunately for Fargo, too many people wanted his attention, and Dora and Lily, elbowed aside, were forced to delay their stinging lecture until some other time. While visiting outlanders and residents of Salt Lake City began making the moonlight journey back to town, Fargo was fed a delicious late-night supper of steak, washed down with hot black coffee and top-grade whiskey. A newspaper reporter perched at his side and wouldn't let him chew a bite in peace.

Fargo noticed Lily riding back with the Emmericks—although she rode in the back of the wagon by herself. Evidently Esther's rage, after catching Lily with him two nights ago, had cooled somewhat. Again Fargo reminded himself that revenge must be her secret goal. Why else would a beautiful woman even want to keep such a job, and in an area she intensely disliked.

As if timed to confuse and worry him more, Dora came near just as Fargo was leading the Ovaro up into an army van—the winning horse always got a ride back to town.

"Skye?"

He glanced down the ramp. "Yeah?"

"I know it's almost eleven o'clock," she said. "And it will be much later before we get back to town. You must be so tired. But could I possibly talk you into coming to my room after we get back?"

Fargo inserted a locking pin through the van's gate and tapped it home with the heel of his palm.

"I thought you were mad at me?" he replied. "Hell, a little while ago you slapped me hard enough to loosen a jaw tooth."

"I *am* mad at you, you prowling tomcat. But never mind that, we need to talk."

"Talk?" Fargo repeated dubiously as he stepped down. Conversation was not his favorite reason for sneaking into a pretty girl's bedroom. "Talk about what?"

"Since you obviously . . . 'know' Lily Snyder, I think you already know what I need to talk with you about. Skye, she's a redhead."

"Hon, it's late and I'm bushed. If you wander near a point, feel free to make it."

"Skye Fargo, you're enough to vex a saint! You know my *point* damn well. Lily is the girl in my peeping stone."

"Must be a tight fit inside that thing," he quipped.

"Will you?" she demanded, ignoring his sarcasm. "Come visit me, I mean?"

Fargo pulled on the point of his chin. "*Just* talk?"

"Well, even though I'm mad at you," she gave in, "I'm not *that* mad. After all, you're not my husband. No vows or promises were broken."

A grin lifted the corner of Fargo's mouth. He *so* admired a reasonable female. "I'll tap on your window as soon as I clean up a mite."

"It overlooks the alley behind the house."

Fargo noticed two men were conspicuously absent tonight and hadn't been here earlier: Frederic Childress and

Cecil McGinnis. Considering how much they had wagered on Stover, it seemed odd they wouldn't be here today to cheer on their investment. Unless they needed every possible second now to cover their asses, knowing their far-flung criminal empire was in danger of crumbling.

Fargo climbed up on the board seat of the van and kept the Mormon driver company back to town. With Micajah's livery burned and gone, Fargo simply led the Ovaro around to the grassy back lot and put him on a long tether. The pinto had already been curried and rubbed down good by volunteers after the race, then grained. For the Ovaro, life hadn't been this plush in some time.

Fargo left his tack and Henry in an unlocked root cellar behind the house. He had no plans to go inside the house right now. Windows in the downstairs parlor were lit up as tenants waited for him and discussed the race.

Instead, he dug a lump of yellowish lye soap from his saddlebag, then worked his way down to City Creek and found a stretch made private by poplars and cottonwoods. Fargo stripped buck, immersed himself in the cool water, lathered, immersed again. In this desert aridity, he required no towel—he was dry a minute after he stepped onto the grassy bank.

Dora answered his first tap on the window, unlatching the casement and swinging it open. Fargo was disappointed to see her fully clothed, complete with shoes and a crisp bonnet.

"I haven't changed my mind," she assured him when she saw the look on his face. "But that night we did it under the stars at Mormon Station—it was wonderful, Skye! Can we do it outside again?"

"Sure, but why, hon? At least there's a bed here."

Even in the dim light, she hid her face from him. "My father always said the best stallions are the ones that neigh the loudest during mating. You're loud, Skye, when the pleasure is on you, and I *like* that. I want us to have plenty of privacy."

Fargo, half of him in the alley behind the Beckmann house, the other half inside Dora's bedroom, liked that idea. Beds were fine things, but walls were often flimsy. Besides, Dora was loud, too.

He lifted her outside, and they headed back toward the same spot where Fargo had just bathed.

"Skye," Dora said as they walked arm in arm under the cottonwoods, "we've *got* to help Lily Snyder."

"Help her how?"

"Well, certainly not the way *you* 'helped' her," Dora snipped. "She's in terrible, terrible trouble, Skye. One week from today, she's going to die if we don't help her."

"Oh, Jesus. You didn't tell *her* all about the 'peeping stone' business, didja?"

Dora shook her pretty head. "I didn't want to scare her or make her think I was crazy. But *she's* the girl from the vision. And no matter how angry I am at you for . . . being with her, I'm *not* mad at Lily. You've got to help her, Skye."

"How? Crawl inside that damn glass bowl?"

Dora slapped his arm. "You think you're so smart, but you don't know neat's-foot! She's in trouble, I tell you."

Fargo fell silent, worrying anew. In fact, "peeping stone" be damned, he agreed with Dora. But he couldn't tell her what he'd guessed about Childress, Lily, and her dead husband. He had no proof, just a wild hunch.

"You could be right," he told her. "I'll see what I can do."

They reached the private spot, and Fargo cut spruce boughs to make a soft bed in the shimmering moonlight. Dora unbuttoned her shoes, pulled off her chemise and pantaloons, then opened her bodice and teased Fargo with her impressive loaves.

Even in the moonlight her nipples were a tantalizing pink color, and already stiff from the cool night breeze. Fargo took one in his mouth and began sucking and, now and then, nipping her with his teeth. She had a clean, pleasant taste like spearmint.

"Oh, my stars, Skye!" she moaned. "It's so nice it makes my legs weak."

"Better lie down, then," he suggested slyly, his own voice husky with lust.

"Good idea, Mr. Trailsman."

She hiked her dress up over her hips and lay back on the bed of boughs, opening her legs for him.

Dora unleashed a keening sound of encouragement as his impressive shaft opened her like a soft, moist fruit. Again and again, until the eastern sky lightened toward dawn, they drove each other to quivering peaks of intense pleasure.

But Fargo knew there was more than an August tenth crisis looming. The death of Dill Stover changed little. Childress and McGinnis were still plotting treachery, and the two Ute renegades were still out there somewhere.

Soon enough, death would once again arrive, searching for his favorite boy, Skye Fargo.

15

"At first," Frederic Childress said on the second day after the Salt Lake Run, busy blotting a sheet of writing with sand, "I thought perhaps we'd overestimated our hirelings. Now I realize we've *under*estimated Fargo. We admired him, yes, but we failed to respect him."

Childress set the sheet down carefully and put a lead paperweight on it.

"It's no different with horses," he said. "Most are pattern buckers. They buck the same way every time, and a rider can anticipate their moves. But a few horses are notional buckers. They buck differently each time. That's Fargo—a notional bucker who, so far, has thrown us."

McGinnis ignored the words, staring at the written sheet. "Is that page your speech for this Saturday?" he demanded, his face incredulous.

"Of course. It's titled 'Christian Charity and the Wild Indian.' You'll need a handkerchief."

McGinnis, pacing nervously in the parlor of his Salt Lake City home, gave a harsh bark of mystified laughter. "Fred, have you gone mad?"

"Not that I'm aware of, but anything's possible."

"My God, man!" McGinnis exclaimed. "You were here yesterday when that goddamn, arrogant Saunders Lee and his soldiers raided this place—on a Sunday, no less—and discovered inflammatory literature in the shed."

Childress waved a negligent hand. "Yes, and that's *all* they found. A few broadsheets. They could have been planted, and no one can prove otherwise. If you were in any serious trouble, do you think I could have bonded you out for twenty dollars? You'll simply be fined."

"It's not just that, Fred. All that money we bet on Stover went right down a rat hole! So did our lucrative mail contract. And Fargo has no intention of loosening the screws on us. Everything else is in jeopardy."

Childress perched on the edge of a big writing desk, watching his partner from those pale-agate eyes that never seemed to blink. "Finally going puny on me, eh, Cecil?"

"My nerve isn't the issue. Things are going to hell fast, for me and you, and if Fargo isn't stopped damn soon there'll be worse than financial loss for us."

"Meaning? . . ."

"Christ, Fred, don't be deliberately dense! There was Orrin Lofley, and all those poison victims scattered around the desert. Stover poisoned those water holes at our orders and everybody knows he worked for you."

Childress flashed a smug, confident smile. "What 'everybody knows' and what can be proven in court are two very different animals."

"Do you really think," McGinnis said, his tone exasperated, "that after finding illegal broadsheets here on my property they won't raid the Mormon Station storehouse? Especially the way Lee has been watching us. And, Fred, once they find that still and those five-hundred rifles, we'll be prison or gallows bound."

"You're an intellectual," Childress replied. "You worry too much because your mind sees all the possibilities for danger. I, in contrast, am a doer. Don't worry about Mormon Station. It will be clean as a whistle before the authorities even arrive."

"Impossible. The world will grow honest first."

"Impossible? It's already happening," Childress assured him. "Do you remember that cache I found in the wilds west of Logan?"

"Yes, but both of us are down here in Salt Lake—"

"Stover"—Childress cut him off—"once introduced me to a man named Deke Stratton. Stratton has a little gang, about a half-dozen rustlers and other owlhoots, who camp with him just north of the Bear River. Anticipating our current troubles some months ago, I met with Stratton. I explained in detail what might have to be hauled out and where to."

"But Bear River is well north of here," McGinnis pointed out. "How will you notify him it's time?"

"That, too, is already done. There's a U.S. Army telegraph station on Bear River. Stratton has telegraphed back—he and his men are on their way to Mormon Station as we speak."

Childress pressed his lips into a wire-tight smile before adding, "So *let* Fargo dash about playing the crusading hero, the hell do we care? That storehouse will be legal by the time the soldiers arrive. And Fargo will look foolish trying to incriminate us with nothing but his pizzle in his hand."

Only a quarter-mile from Cecil McGinnis's home, at the barracks housing the Mormon Battalion, Skye Fargo and Captain Saunders Lee were conferring at the same time as Childress and his partner.

"I still can't believe it, Skye," Saunders said yet again. "But there it is, in black and white. You could soon be a rich man if you chose to."

"Hell, I am rich," Fargo replied. "I have two hundred fifty dollars in brand-new gold shiners. Plus the dollar you're going to give me for the contract. That buck'll get me into a poker game."

The two men had met in Saunders's cramped bachelor officer's quarters, a low-ceilinged, windowless room only twelve feet by fifteen feet. Fargo stood studying a wall map of the Utah Territory. He suddenly remembered seeing Saunders and Lily together on the night of the Salt Lake Run.

"Anyway," he added, "it's worth it to see you get hitched. I still can't believe Captain Spit 'n' Polish has got himself a sweetheart. What's next—holidays in hell?"

"Ah, go pee up a rope, Lothario. Sure, I back-trailed from women most of my life while you were counting coup on them. But L—" Saunders caught himself just in time. "This lady, I mean, is the fairest flower of all the fields, and all that poetic stuff."

Fargo watched his friend from the corner of one eye. He had heard that 'l' sound when Saunders almost accidentally named his lady. 'L' for Lily? *Damn*, he thought, *did I make whoopee with Saunders's girl?*

But much more ominous than the sexual dalliance, if Lily really *was* Saunders's girl: the officer might be on the verge of losing her. Even lacking proof, Fargo was almost convinced she had something reckless planned for next Saturday when Childress spoke. All the signs pointed that way, and Fargo was an expert sign reader.

"Skye," Saunders said, studying the map with him, "if we don't stop these troublemakers like Childress and McGinnis, stop them *soon*, this area is going to end up like Parker County, Texas, where marauding Comanches have decimated the population. We're greatly outnumbered here."

Fargo nodded. "Indians are trouble enough without getting them all jollified on liquor."

"Hunh, don't *we* know? I still have nightmares about those Cheyenne Dog Soldiers who got hold of that whiskey shipment in the Niobrara River country. I'm also looking ahead, Skye. A lot depends on the harvest around here."

"Tribute?" Skye asked.

Saunders nodded. "Exactly. If we can afford to feed the Utes, that should ease the trouble. But a drought is on, and if we don't get rain soon, the harvest may be a disaster."

Fargo said nothing to this because Saunders had enough on his mind. But Fargo had learned to accurately forecast rain by studying spiderwebs. A long and thin web indicated a dry spell. Short and thick meant rain. And the last one he had examined was *very* long and thin.

"Never mind the Indians for now," Fargo suggested. "Go after the still and the criminals who run it."

"I'm trying," Saunders replied. "This morning I sent out twenty troopers provisioned and armed for fifteen days in the field. They have a list of possible grogshop locations."

"Won't do any good," Fargo insisted. "Too much dust and clinking of bit chains. Regular troops are damn near worthless in the desert. Think about it. It would require a good-sized still to supply all those grogshops. My money is on Mormon Station. Childress has a big storehouse there."

"And if that storehouse houses nothing illegal," Saunders pointed out, "Brigham Young will wear my guts for garters. This wouldn't be a legal raid with a territorial warrant— that lets too many people warn them it's coming, and Childress keeps informers everywhere. Only a surprise raid would work, and we both know that means a very small force."

"That rings right," Fargo said. "It could be done by three, make that four, men with a scaling ladder to clear the outer wall."

"It's four days to Mormon Station," Saunders said, "but that's by slow-moving oxen. It's much less than two days on a swift horse."

Fargo thought about that and the fact that he wanted to be back in Salt Lake City by this Saturday, August tenth, for the Childress lecture. He tried to convince himself Dora's "peeping stone" nonsense had nothing to do with his returning, just the real evidence and clues.

"Swift horses, you say? Horses like ours?" Fargo asked, and Saunders grinned his answer.

"This is Monday," Fargo added. "I need to be back here in five days."

"So do I," Saunders reminded him. "I'll be in charge of security next Saturday at the lecture hall."

"All right, if we're going to throw the net around Childress and McGinnis, I say let's get it done," Fargo urged. "Hell, let's leave tonight if we can. I don't much like two-faced sons of bitches who hire jobbers to kill me."

"Childress and McGinnis," Saunders repeated, shaking his head in amazement. "Skye, those two are a dangerous new element out here. There were plenty of Mormons on hand when gold was discovered at Sutter's mill back in forty-eight. Instead of cashing in on the easy pickings, they went home to Deseret. McGinnis is a phony Mormon."

"Yeah. Like Childress, he's part of this damned get-rich-quick crowd," Fargo agreed. " 'The sun travels west and so does opportunity.' It's cash in and get out, the damage to others be damned. Their breed strip the hills of trees and soil, then level the hills themselves. They flood entire valleys and ruin twenty poor families to help one rich one get richer. And the ones like Childress and McGinnis don't even work hard to steal. They just hire out the cold-blooded killing."

Fargo glanced at the slant of the sun on the floor near the open door.

"Got to git," he told Saunders, clapping his hat back on. "As you know, soldier boy, night riding is easier in this salt desert. Are we dusting our hocks north to Mormon Station or not?"

Saunders gave that a sarcastic laugh. "Since when do you ask my permission to raise six sorts of hell any damn time or place you choose?"

But the remark was to hide his hesitancy. Fargo understood his dilemma. Even though he was soon resigning his commission, he'd still be held responsible for anything that went wrong.

"Your stallion is rested from the race?" his friend asked. "It's only been two days."

"That pinto is death to the devil."

"All right," Saunders decided. "I'll stop by your boardinghouse after supper. I'll bring short rations and ammo."

"Don't overdo the ammo," Fargo advised. "I didn't see any guards up there. It shouldn't turn into a big shooting match."

Saunders grinned. "Famous last words."

Esther Emmerick had gradually calmed down after her near hysteria when she caught Fargo and Lily in his room, both virtually naked. In truth, she was proud to have such a fabled man as Fargo in her establishment. It brought in extra customers for breakfast and dinner.

Nonetheless, Fargo had taken care since that night not to have Lily in his room nor to visit hers. But he had noticed something odd—Lily often waited, until very late at night, other times soon after sunset, then sneaked quietly down the seldom-used back stairs of the house.

On Monday evening, as Fargo sat in his room cleaning and oiling his weapons, he heard a step on the stairs that ended near his window. The newly replaced window stood open. First he made sure the yard was clear, then he poked his head out and saw Lily Snyder in the grainy twilight.

"I've twigged your game," he greeted her bluntly. "Or part of it, anyhow."

Even in that stingy light she seemed to pale. But that distracting smile of hers was quickly in place.

"What 'game' would that be, Skye?" she said with what seemed feigned confusion.

"Frederic Childress, next Saturday at Civic Lecture Hall. I think you mean to kill him."

Her laughter, too, seemed forced, to Fargo. "*Kill* him? But I'm a fellow outlander."

"Kill him, sure. That's why you've got the gun, the one you're carrying in your pocket right now. I'd wager that Childress water-starved your husband, and somehow you found out. Now you mean to settle accounts. I don't blame you, and the son of a bitch deserves it. But not if it's going to ruin your life, and it damn sure will."

"Skye . . . your concern is sweet, but all this is just absurd! Check with the officials—no one will be permitted inside the hall without a ticket. I don't *have* a ticket. Outlanders need a sponsor, and I have none."

Fargo said stubbornly, "Then you mean to kill him going in or coming out."

"Impossible. Soldiers will be everywhere, Skye."

Fargo was silent now, watching her in the dim light. Her points were well taken, he had to admit it. But she seemed to rattle them off too glibly, like someone who'd practiced.

"Where you headed now?" he asked.

"To meet somebody," she said coyly.

Again that tight nubbin of doubt was back in Fargo's stomach. Was she meeting with Saunders before the officer came here to meet up with Fargo for the ride north? Hell, Fargo wouldn't care one red cent about it except it was going to make it tough to look Saunders in the eye from now on. There weren't that many outlanders in Salt Lake, let alone young and pretty females. Yet, there was that damned "l" sound when he almost named his secret girl.

"Lily," he said, "are you *sure* you don't have a Mormon beau? Anyone even squiring you around?"

This time her musical laughter sounded genuine. Fargo whiffed her hyacinth perfume and had a pleasant memory of their bare skin rubbing.

"Don't you think I'd know if I did, Skye?"

She would, Fargo agreed, unless Saunders hadn't stated his feelings to her yet. Fargo recalled Saunders's words from last week: *Tell you the truth, I haven't said much to her yet about how I feel.*

"Shit," Fargo muttered.

"I beg your pardon?"

"Nothing, sorry."

After Lily had gone, Fargo finished cleaning his weapons, then ran a whetstone over the blade of his Arkansas Toothpick.

Out back, the Ovaro suddenly whinnied his bear-grease signal. Fargo cursed, having crossed this river once before, then blew out the lamp. He positioned himself to one side of the window, putting solid wall to his back.

He eased out his Colt, pulling the hammer to half-cock. The curtains stirred, hands groped inside. Fargo started taking up the trigger slack.

A head edged into the room, raggedly cut dark hair held back by a leather band. Fargo couldn't miss the pungent odor of bear grease. The moment he saw a raised weapon, that red son was headed for the Forest of Tears.

"Far-go. Far-go! I am He Bear, one of the Utes you defeat two sleeps ago in Spanish Canyon. I would speak with you."

He Bear jumped when Fargo spoke from right beside him. "Who else is with you?"

"Nothing but Trouble. We have both left our weapons back with our ponies. I swear this thing."

"I believe you," Fargo said, still holding his gun. "But I'm the careful type. Especially with you two. Tell your pard to show both his hands, too."

But the other Ute heard and showed his hands. Fargo had them back up slow, keeping their hands in view, while he followed them into the back lot that quickly turned into open desert. Fargo didn't bother asking them into his room—few mountain Utes, or any other wild Indians, would abide a closed room.

"You have words for my ears?" Fargo invited.

"This Childress," He Bear said, contempt stamped into his features. "Never—*never* could he have borne what you bore in Spanish Canyon. Yet, we have done this cowardly dog's bidding while he insults us."

"Is it true," Nothing but Trouble put in, "these things we learn from our runners and smoke and mirror signals? How you have crossed lances with Childress?"

The "moccasin telegraph"—Fargo wasn't surprised. Sometimes it was quicker and more accurate than the white man's talking wire.

"I'm on his trail," Fargo confirmed. "If you two really hate him so much, stop helping him."

"We mean to help him *die*," He Bear said passionately. "He has caused the death of many, red and white. That is why we are here. To seek your permission to kill him."

Fargo almost grinned in the moonlight. These gents would have to get in line, apparently, behind Lily. Before he could answer the Utes, a horse trotted around the back corner of the house.

Fargo recognized the big gray.

"It's all right," he told the nervous Utes. "He's a soldier but he's my friend."

Saunders didn't look any too happy at the sight of Utes in his city after dark. But he was civil when Fargo introduced the three men to each other.

"Where's those other two soldiers?" Fargo asked. "Waiting around front?"

"Uh, yeah, about that . . ." Saunders dismounted, his face twisting with anger and resentment. "My executive officer doesn't like the mission. Most he would do is give me temporary additional duty time—until Saturday. Means I can drop my regular duties and take on a special mission."

"I don't like it," Fargo said immediately. "If there *is* a guard, we'll need good covering fire on that scaling ladder. We better forget—"

Fargo fell silent as his eyes hesitated on the Utes. *Hell, why not?* Volunteers were always best, and Utes were certainly good scrappers. Not to mention excellent riders and nighttime fighters. Their gripe against Childress ought to help, too.

Fargo explained the mission to the Utes while Saunders looked like he was choking on a chicken bone.

"These two would rather have a chance to kill Childress," Fargo told his friend. "But they'd be happy as all hell to go along on this mission to destroy his interests. That jake with you?"

Saunders, watching the Utes skeptically, lowered his voice. "I don't know, Skye. This could even be an elaborate scheme hatched by Childress. These two could kill us at any time."

"Possibility," Fargo agreed. "But these ain't strangers, these two. I've met them before."

At this intelligence, Saunders perked up considerably. "Ah! You'll vouch for them, then?"

"Hell yes. They damn near killed me," Fargo assured him, laughing when the officer's eyes widened.

16

Fargo, Saunders, and the two Utes headed north on Monday night. A full moon, and the nighttime coolness of the desert, allowed them to make impressive time until sunrise.

They paused, on Tuesday morning, for a two-hour rest. Then it was back in the saddle again.

"Those damn Utes," Fargo muttered to Saunders, taking his hat off to dry his sweaty hair. "Always showing off."

He Bear and Nothing but Trouble sat their ponies out ahead, patiently waiting for the slower palefaces.

"No wonder my men can't ever catch them," Saunders replied, spurring his gray forward.

Fargo caught up with him. "You ain't said yet how we're gonna work this at Mormon Station," he told his friend. "I figure it'll be broad daylight tomorrow when we arrive. But is it a good idea to enter that storehouse in front of witnesses?"

"Nix on that, Skye. I have no key, so we'll have to force our way in. That'll be all right if we find proof of high crimes against the territory and seize it. The military isn't bound by the civilian legal code, so the proof is all that matters. But if that place is clean, I'd like a chance to slip out unseen. That way, the only crime is a broken lock."

Fargo nodded. "So we go in after dark. That's better, anyway. By now Childress and McGinnis have had time to put guards out. I prefer night fighting."

"Besides," Saunders added dryly, "I doubt if the residents of Mormon Station would be overjoyed to see a pair of tough Ute warriors come riding in."

"Especially," Fargo said, "after the good job Childress and McGinnis have done of whipping up anti-Indian senti-

151

ment out here. They work both sides of it: they sell the Indians spiked-up liquor that no man could drink without going loco. Then they goad the white man by trumpeting the 'Indian atrocities.' Not that all red sons are scrubbed angels."

They rested for two hours after sunset, then rode straight through again that night. By noon Wednesday the four tired men and horses had reached the sandstone rises west of Mormon Station—the very spot where Dill Stover tried, eleven days ago, to hurl Fargo into eternity.

"What now, Captain?" Fargo asked, lake-blue eyes slitted as he studied the verdant Salt Lake Valley with its patchwork of fields. Fargo was used to taking charge himself in these situations. But Captain Saunders Lee was the official authority in Deseret as well as a damn good field commander.

"We make a cold camp up on the rises," Saunders said. "We sleep until dark, then we scale the wall in the corner farthest from the guard bastions."

Fargo nodded; the Utes, as usual, looked stoic and indifferent, their faces as passive as granite slabs. The four men rode atop the rises, following a narrow and winding ledge. Saunders knew this entire territory and quickly led them to a cool sand cave big enough for men and horses. Fargo grained and watered the Ovaro, spent some time removing pebbles from the pinto's hoofs with a blunt nail. Then he cleaned the blow sand from his weapons. After a forgettable meal of stale hardtack and salted beef, he spread his groundsheet and blanket and fell promptly asleep.

Sometime later a hand gripped his shoulder, and Fargo's Colt appeared even before he was fully awake.

"I'm too young and handsome to die, Skye." Saunders's voice reached Fargo's ears. "Shoot one of the Indians—they smell ripe."

Fargo's eyes eased open, and he saw his Colt was tucked into Saunders's belly. "Sorry, old son. I told you before, don't touch me when you wake me up."

The Utes, looking well rested, were already mounted and patiently waiting outside the cave. Fargo could tell, from the position and color of the moon, that it was around 10 P.M. That was plenty late in any frontier town, let alone a Mormon community.

They rode down into the valley at a trot, then switched to a walk to cut noise. About a quarter of a mile outside the high wall, they hobbled their horses in thick shadows and proceeded on foot, Fargo carrying the scaling ladder.

Fargo had learned over the years that when a mission like this looked too easy, that meant it would end up being a world of misery. And, at first, it was too easy.

Not one shout was raised as all four raiders laid their ladder against the wall and climbed over, Fargo last and pulling the ladder over with him. Saunders, who had brought along a strong jimmy, had the door of the big storehouse open within minutes.

"Clean!" Saunders pronounced in a vastly disappointed voice after a quick glance around by the light of a torch. "Damnit, Skye, looks like we were wrong."

Fargo shook his head. It was true that everything now stacked in the building seemed legal: canned food, footwear and clothing, cookware. But appearances were deceiving.

"Whiff that air," he told Saunders. "At first I thought it was just the strong alfalfa smell in this area. But whiff deep."

Saunders sampled a deep lungful. "Mash!"

Fargo nodded. "There was a big still in here until recently. And the alfalfa smell outside covered it."

He went back outside and slowly circled the storehouse, at times holding his face almost on the ground to study the signs.

"Those tracks outside are easy to read," he told Saunders when he came back inside. "Somebody in two conveyances moved the incriminating stuff out. And the dirt inside the tracks is still flat and hard-pressed. In a desert, wheel tracks crumble after twenty-four hours or so. Whoever took this stuff couldn't have left more than a day ago."

Saunders furrowed his brow, trying to study this out. "Meaning somebody here works for Childress and let them in and out of the gate."

"Finding that person is small potatoes, right now," Fargo said. "The names will come out."

"Yeah. Skye, you and I need to be back in Salt Lake City by Saturday. But these men are obviously moving in slow conveyances. I think we should cut sign on them and see if we can cross their trail."

"That shines," Fargo agreed. "Without that contraband, our case against Childress and McGinnis ain't worth a busted tug chain. Let's get thrashing."

Deke Stratton was a wiry, compact man, deceptively mild and courteous in appearance. Unlike many hardcases on the frontier, he always shaved regularly and wore the clean range duds of a cowboy. He knew that a scruffy beard and greasy clothing were outlaw markers to lawmen.

"How's it look on our back-trail, A.J.?" he asked the man who'd just ridden into their camp forty miles east of Mormon Station.

"Not even a coyote pup stirring, boss. This job is like stealing a bird's nest off the ground."

Stratton nodded but said nothing, idly scratching behind the ears of a big yellow cur he took along with him everywhere. Two freight wagons stood tongue-to-tailgate in the moonlight, heaped high with contraband that meant serious prison time if seized in the Utah Territory: wooden crates of repeating rifles, all the parts for a massive still, stolen military rations.

"Easy or not," he finally told A.J., "it's best to go wake up the boys. If a cool-nerved bastard like Fred Childress is scared, that means there must be a fly in the ointment. Let's just keep pushing east until we've got the stuff hidden."

"Jesus, boss, my balls are sore from pounding a saddle! Can't we just wait until—"

"No, we can't. That heavy rain earlier did a nice job of wiping out our trail for a stretch. But we didn't allow for the mud-caked wheels slowing us down. We're behind schedule, and I don't like sitting out here waiting for trouble to find us. Not with *this* load."

"If trouble finds us," A.J. said grimly as he left to kick the boys awake, "trouble will find more trouble."

Stratton agreed. Most of his men were experienced rustlers, and thus, old hands at moving and fighting in the dark. The five men with him now were top hands with a gun and no strangers to shooting scrapes.

Stratton would avoid gunplay if he could. But he was a wanted man, and if it came down to a cartridge session, damn straight there would be *no* surrender from his side.

*   *   *

At first, even in moonlight, the tracks Fargo's group were following were so clear a blind hog could have held the trail. The secretive freighters were headed due east, toward Logan.

By dawn, however, the trail reached a stretch of ground that had been washed by heavy rain, and the trail disappeared. But Fargo, sure their quarry was headed toward Logan, simply held their present course for several miles on a hunch. Sure enough, like magic the trail resumed on the other side of the washout.

Fargo rode out alone, after sunrise Thursday morning, on advance scout. He couldn't help thinking, *Only two days now to make it back to Salt Lake City.* The slightest delay meant he wouldn't be there when Lily Snyder did whatever the hell she had planned for Childress.

Thus preoccupied, Fargo almost foolishly gave himself away when he topped a long sandstone ridge and spotted the men below. He counted two freight wagons and six well-armed men with as many saddle horses.

"Almost time to open the ball," he muttered to the Ovaro as he wheeled him around and headed back.

"Listen, both of you," Saunders warned both Utes after Fargo gave his report. "We can't just wipe them out. As a soldier I'm required to give them a chance to surrender."

"Wrong men for this," was all He Bear said.

Fargo, however, was not so diplomatic. He shook his head.

"Saunders, it may be the law," he said, "but it's not a smart idea. Deke Stratton is only a fox step ahead of a murder warrant. And most of his men are wanted for something. They'll fight like cornered Apaches."

"The law is the law, Skye. If *I* don't respect it, who will?"

"You're talking sense," Fargo said reluctantly. "That's why I'm not a soldier. That, and the unbearable shortage of women."

Because the loaded vehicles were lumbering along so slowly, Fargo and his group caught them well before midmorning.

This terrain, east of the Great Salt Lake, was not so barren, and Stratton's gang had stopped in a copse of poplars and silver spruce. One of the wagons had thrown an iron tire, and two men were busy warping it back onto the wooden wheel.

"You three stay back," Saunders told Fargo and the Utes. "We'll try this by the book first. After all, these men are only transporting the stuff, they don't face serious charges if they surrender."

"Not a good idea," Fargo repeated. "But you're an idealist, God help you, and I admire that in a man. I'll back your foolish play, you blockhead."

Saunders rode out a few hundred feet until he was in plain view of the men below.

"Hallo, the copse!" he shouted. "This is Captain Saunders Lee of the Mormon Battalion. You are all under arrest for transporting contraband items. Throw down your weapons and hold your hands out in plain view."

Only seconds later the men below gave their emphatic answer in lead, a sudden volley of shots making a crackling sound. Saunders's plumed hat flew off just before his horse folded to the ground dead, almost trapping the officer's legs.

Fargo and the Utes opened up, sending down a swarm of hot lead to take the pressure off Saunders while he escaped on foot. Below, in the copse, bushes rattled and shook, divots of earth flew everywhere, chunks of bark went spinning off the trees.

At least one man below looked dead, shot in the initial volley. But the other five were giving a good account of themselves, keeping things lively up on the ridge where Fargo was ducking death. The air fairly hummed with bullets.

"They mean to fight to the death!" a crouching Fargo shouted to his companions. "So why sit up here until our ammo is gone? The best way to cure a boil is to lance it."

"You're saying we should charge them?" Saunders said.

"Sure. They don't expect just four of us to do that. We charge on foot to make smaller targets, me and you from this direction, He Bear and Nothing but Trouble from the flanks. It might get us all killed, but who wants to live forever?"

"Another suicide charge conceived by Skye Fargo,"

Saunders joked. "I'm going to heaven, anyway, so let's try it."

With a roar to nerve themselves, the two friends went flying down the ridge, weapons blazing, while the Utes moved stealthily to the flanks.

"Zig and zag!" Fargo urged as the air around them turned metallic and deadly.

Their gutsy move had obviously caught Stratton and his gang flat-footed. One man, firing from the bed of a wagon, caught a bullet in his forehead and pitched over the sideboards like a sack of garbage.

"Four left!" Fargo shouted.

A bullet spun Fargo's hat around, and the acrid stench of burned powder saturated the area. A head poked out from behind a wheel, and Fargo shot from the hip with his Henry, scoring a lethal hit.

"Three left!" Saunders shouted. "Lucky hit, Fargo!"

By now Stratton, who was firing from behind one of the wagons, was as scared as his two surviving men. The Utes had opened up with their revolving-cylinder rifles, and deadly fire was hitting the men from three directions.

Fargo knew that Stratton was the neat-looking one furiously working the lever of a Volcanic rifle. But he couldn't drop a bead on him without rounding behind that freight wagon. Gunfire exploding continuously now, he tore around the tailgate of the big wagon, Henry cocked and at the ready.

With a vicious snarl, a huge yellow wolf-dog leaped onto Fargo from seemingly nowhere. The Trailsman was knocked down hard, the Henry flying from his hands.

"Fargo, your next camp will be in hell!" Stratton gloated triumphantly, standing right over the dazed and helpless man and pointing his rifle dead center on Fargo's lights.

It happened in mere moments, and Fargo had no time to react. He Bear, seeing this and out of bullets, raised a yipping war cry and rushed forward, thrusting his lance. Stratton howled like a torture victim when the stone tip ripped into him low, exposing pink entrails.

The next second, however, Fargo's stomach sank when one of the two surviving men killed He Bear. In an eyeblink, Fargo's Henry was smoking again. He, Nothing but

Trouble, and Saunders were able to quickly kill the other two.

Fargo tried to apologize to Nothing but Trouble for the death of his heroic friend. But the Ute would have none of it.

"He Bear warrior like you, Far-go. Him knew risks. When does Far-go ever fail to protect friend in battle? Every brave Ute dream of dying in glorious battle. Saving man like you, man with powerful medicine, mean He Bear will be honored in the Land Beyond the Sun."

They buried He Bear, burning gun powder over the grave to discourage predators. Nothing but Trouble was visibly impressed when Fargo knife-slashed one of his own arms and let it bleed on the grave, the traditional Indian sign of mourning.

"It's two days to Logan," Saunders told Fargo, pulling out his watch and thumbing back the cover. "We need to haul this evidence there so I can leave it under military guard. But I don't think that's going to leave us enough time to get back to Salt Lake City early enough on Saturday."

Fargo was already heading upslope to retrieve his Ovaro. "We'll make it," he replied, thinking of foolish, pretty Lily. "We don't have any choice."

17

Stratton's now defunct gang had cut the telegraph wires behind them as they fled, not forgetting the trunk line that included Mormon Station. Thus, nothing could be reported to Salt Lake City. Captain Saunders Lee was unable to order the immediate arrest of Childress. It would have to wait until their arrival in Salt Lake City.

The Salt Lake Run had been a Sunday stroll compared to the grueling ride from Logan to Salt Lake. Nothing but Trouble parted from them about halfway, heading toward the Wasatch and the big mountain Ute camp there. Saunders, his best horse dead, had selected one of the outlaw mounts, a blaze-faced sorrel that hadn't been used too badly.

Even so, the horse began to flag about six hours north of Salt Lake. The Ovaro, however, still had plenty of bottom left.

"I'm going on ahead," Fargo told him. "I have to be back before sunrise."

"Wait, *I'm* the one needs to be there by sunrise. Mainly to arrest Childress at the lecture hall. Why you?"

Because at midnight it'll be August tenth, Fargo thought. *And a grieving but foolish young woman needs to be protected from herself.*

"You said *by* sunrise, I said *before*. Besides, I don't want to miss Esther's fine breakfast," was all Fargo told Saunders before he kicked the Ovaro up to a gallop.

"Skye! Skye, what the—"

Fargo ignored him, for he wasn't about to reveal anything to Saunders that might get Lily jailed—or ruin his romance with her, if she was Saunders's secret love.

Salt Lake City was dark and still when Fargo arrived about two hours before dawn, prowling wolves scattering before him. In his room, he quickly scrubbed off the top layer of trail dust, leaving mud in the basin. Then Fargo headed up the outside stairs to Lily's garret at the top of the steps.

Despite the hour, an oily yellow glow filled the window. Fargo swept a curtain aside and peeked in. Lily, fully dressed in black bombazine, sat on the edge of her narrow mattress, evidently praying silently.

A Christian Bible was in her left hand, a Colt Pocket Model in her right.

"Damn," Fargo muttered, "this girl's flying the black flag."

He rapped on the windowsill, and Lily nearly fell off the bed in fright.

"Don't shoot, it's just that lovable Trailsman," Fargo said cheerfully as he invited himself in.

"Skye! I . . . what are you doing here? It's not even four o'clock."

He nodded, eyes darting around the small but neat room. "Four o'clock," he repeated. "And you wide awake, dressed in widow's weeds. Imagine my surprise."

"It's not mourning clothes, silly. I just chose a sober black dress to shut Esther up."

"Reading the Bible, at this time of night," he said, "doesn't need to be explained. But I'm sure curious about that gun. You got rats?"

"It just makes me feel better to have it close by. What good is a gun that's packed at the bottom of a trunk?"

Fargo laughed, spun a ladderback chair around backward, straddled it. "Well, now you got *me* close by. Feel even better?"

A look of panic flitted across Lily's pale, finely boned face. "I . . . I plan on going back to bed."

Fargo grinned. *Sure* she did. "I'm flexible," he assured her.

"Skye! After we were caught in your room, you—"

"Spare me the indignant female stuff. I didn't come up here for slap and tickle, nice as that would be."

"Then what are you doing here?" she demanded.

Fargo shrugged. "Whatever you want, though I'm no Bible reader. Got any cards or dominoes?"

"You mean, you're really staying here, uninvited? How long?"

"Oh," Fargo replied casually, "until Fred Childress gives his lecture and leaves."

"I have no idea what you're talking about."

"Sure, and Queen Victoria is my sweetheart."

"If you must impose on me," Lily groused, "would you like a glass of whiskey?"

"I've been known to taste it."

But in fact Fargo hadn't tasted hard spirits since the mash he'd drunk with Micajah Jones two days before the race. While Lily turned away to pour it from a decanter on the highboy, Fargo loosened his heavy gun belt and hung it over the back of the chair.

Unbidden, the image of He Bear's remote, lonely grave came to Fargo, and his throat tightened. But the Trailsman was proud to also recall the warrior's last, glorious charge into furious fire.

"You know, Lily," he said, "plenty have died at Childress's order, plenty besides your husband. It's not just *your* responsibility to kill him."

"Whatever fantastic plans you suspect I have," she said, handing Fargo a pony glass filled to the brim with shimmering topaz liquor, "you're just wrong."

Fargo drained half the glass. "Frederic Childress," he replied, "sells water to people in the desert. Fifteen dollars a glass. If you don't have the money, you die. Your husband, Jimmy, didn't have the money, did he?"

Despite her efforts to look incredulous, a tear spurted from one of Lily's eyes and zigzagged down her cheek.

"No," she finally admitted. "He didn't. But the kind person who found Jimmy's body along the California Trail sent me his personal possessions. Including a note he managed to scrawl explaining what happened."

Fargo nodded, a bit sluggishly. That long damn horseback ride must be catching up with him, he thought idly—his eyelids suddenly felt heavy.

"Hell, I don't blame you for the way you feel," he told her, yawning wide. "But do you think Jimmy wrote that note hoping *you* would be placed in danger by it?"

"Of course not, but I don't care. He was my husband, and I loved him, still do. There's no legal proof of what

Childress did, but I *can't* just let him get away with murder."

"That scum bucket will get his," Fargo assured her, yawning again.

"I suppose you're right," Lily said, watching him closely now.

"We'll just . . . stay here," Fargo muttered, his head dropping onto his folded arms on the back of the chair. "Wait until . . . Childress . . ."

Lily had added a stiff dose of laudanum to Fargo's whiskey. As he began to slump out of the chair, she caught him under both arms. He was too big and heavy to haul over to the bed, so she simply lowered him to the floor and tucked a pillow under his head.

"Skye Fargo," she said softly, "you are a brave and noble man. I'll never forget your kindness and what you tried to do for me. But Childress *will* pay, that snake-eyed, stone-hearted bastard."

She blew out the lamp, placed her Colt in a dress pocket, and headed out her window for what was probably the last time. Before this morning was over, she'd either be dead or in prison—and, frankly, Lily was rooting for death.

Exhausted and drugged as he was, Fargo would have slept until at least midmorning if there hadn't been a sudden, loud thumping on the door.

"Lilian!" Esther's rusted-metal voice squawked through the door. "Time to get up! We have dozens of window shades to clean today. And *don't* get yourself up like a hussy!"

Fargo heard the words, but for perhaps twenty seconds they failed to make sense. He had no idea where he was except that he was lying on a split-slab floor, and a window over his head showed the new light of day.

Day . . . Lily . . .

"God*damn*it! She doped me!"

Head still thick with sleep fumes, Fargo sprang to his feet, buckled on his gun belt, and ran down the back steps. Even though he didn't know Lily's exact plan, obviously she meant to shoot her husband's killer, and that meant she had to be in the vicinity of Civic Lecture Hall, located between the forks of City Creek.

Mormon soldiers ringed the building, and Fargo glimpsed Saunders near the front door.

"Have you seen Lily Snyder?" Fargo demanded.

The officer, who'd barely made it back in time, looked both weary and perplexed. "Lily? Why would she be here?"

"Never mind, for the moment," Fargo said, heading around to the back door. "But if you see her, Saunders, take her into custody immediately, without warning her."

If she was in the audience, Fargo figured, Saunders would have seen her. But she had to be here somewhere. He took a quick look around and found a narrow stairwell nearly hidden by some curtains. As he headed up the dark steps, he could hear the droning of Childress's voice out front.

A swing-down ladder led up into an attic. As Fargo climbed up hand over hand, he could now make out the words of the speech: ". . . the American Indian is one of the last great examples of Rousseau's noble savage . . ."

The audible *snick* of a gun being cocked, just above him, made Fargo's blood ice. He practically leaped up the last few rungs.

Childress droned on: ". . . these morally pure 'bachelors of the forest' deserve all the Christian charity of any other . . ."

Fargo's head shot through the opening into a little crawl space lighted by one candle. Lily, hunched over, was listening to Childress, her face carved with hatred.

"You dirty bastard," he heard her mutter, and then before she even realized Fargo was there, she threw back a bolt.

"Lily!" Fargo said desperately, diving forward.

He had glimpsed the hinged board covered with wax receptacles, and the odor told him the thick red liquid inside them was paint. But at the moment, the hinged panel was about to plunge open. Fargo made a desperate grab and caught one corner of it just in time to stop it.

"Damn you, Skye!"

Lily made a choking sound of desperation and aimed her Colt Pocket Model at Fargo. One arm aching from holding the damn heavy panel, Fargo had no choice: he used his free hand to clip Lily on the jaw and knock her out.

She revived a few moments later. Before she could protest, Fargo pressed a finger to her lips. "Before you have a hissy fit, watch this."

Fargo held the hinged panel open just enough to give them both a view of the auditorium below with its varnished speaker's dais up front and Childress in a fancy gray suit and crisp linen. Abruptly, smack in the middle of the hypocritical speech, Saunders Lee's clear, resonant voice shouted from the doorway, "Childress, you are under military arrest for high crimes against the people of Utah Territory! Do not attempt to flee, the hall is surrounded."

Saunders had wanted a highly public arrest, to send a clear warning to others, Mormon or outlander. But, evidently, Childress knew arrest was the end of the road, for him. Fargo saw him whip out a Colt Navy and fire at Saunders, then turn and literally dive out of the nearest window.

But Mormon soldiers were trained to follow orders, and flight was evidence of guilt—before Childress could even get to his feet, at least a dozen troops shot him to ribbons—all visible to the couple up in the attic. Childress died hard, screaming in agony as his body bullet-danced like a man having a seizure.

Moments later, Cecil McGinnis, seated in the audience, was clamped in double irons and led across the street to the military stockade.

"Satisfied?" Fargo asked Lily.

"He's dead," she said softly. "I got to see him die an awful death, and I won't be going to prison. Oh, *yes,* I'm satisfied, Skye Fargo. It won't give me Jimmy back, but Childress will do no more killing."

This time the tears spurting down her face came from the well of joy. "Thanks to you, Skye, I won't have to go to prison—or worse. I not only want to get on with my life, finally, but I *have* a life to get on with. How could I ever repay you?"

Fargo grinned slyly as they headed toward the ladder. "Hmm . . . that's a stumper, innit? Just *how* can a pretty gal show her gratitude to Skye Fargo? Well, maybe we'll think of something, huh?"

*   *   *

Within a week of the arrest of Childress and McGinnis, not one grogshop was operating within the vast Utah Territory. Nor were poison water holes cropping up anywhere.

The Mormon school year began in August, and John Beckmann quickly became the popular new teacher at the grammar school. Fargo's final visit to the Beckmanns found Estelline growing strong and the four kids feisty as ever. Dora, meantime, had turned the head of a gentile banker headed for San Francisco. They were soon to be married.

A truly awkward moment arrived, for Fargo, when Saunders Lee spotted him about a week after the death of Childress.

"Skye!" came his voice from a hansom cab on Commerce Street.

Saunders, wearing civilian clothing, leaped out. "It's official, old friend. I resigned my commission and, thanks to you, I'm going into the mail service. Now that everything's out in the open, I'd like you to finally meet my bride-to-be."

Oh, shit, Fargo thought as Saunders reached a hand into the closed vehicle. *Here it comes.*

"She's been working at Emmerick's boardinghouse," Saunders now felt free to divulge, and Fargo experienced the final despair of the damned. So it *was* Lily all along.

A sweet little blonde with a pug nose popped into view.

"Louise Ahearn, meet Skye Fargo," Saunders said proudly. "Louise is the cook at your boardinghouse. She's another California Trail widow like Lily Snyder. We met when I rescued her in the desert."

"And I stayed," she added, "because of Saunders. Thank you, Mr. Fargo, for helping us get started."

Fargo, an ear-to-ear smile dividing his face, wished them well.

A few days later Fargo rode out of Salt Lake City, heading up toward Pikes Peak country to find work as a hunter. As he rode down Seventh Street, Dora stepped into the dusty street holding her "peeping stone" so he couldn't miss it.

"Should I take a peek," she teased him, "see what's in store for you?"

Fargo turned ashen when she stared at that damned hoodoo glass.

"None of your damn parlor tricks," he replied. "Put that thing away."

She laughed and ran closer for a final kiss. "I thought you didn't put any faith in such foolishness?"

Fargo didn't. Yet he had to admit it—there was plenty of "strange history" that would die with him, unrecorded but still real. And Dora's fantastic "peeping stone" was now part of that history.

Fargo tossed Dora a final wave, slipped the riding thong over his Colt, and pointed the Ovaro's bridle due east toward the Rocky Mountains.

*Texas, 1860—where twisting trails are filled with
deception and danger*

The woman—or trouble?

That was the question Skye Fargo had to ask himself as
he stood at the bar of the Fort Worth saloon and sipped
from a mug of beer.

Of course, philosophically speaking, women often *were*
trouble, Fargo thought, but at the moment he wasn't interested in philosophy. His attention was directed more
toward the long, midnight-black hair and graceful yet sen-
suous curves of the young woman who stood next to him.

He had ridden into Fort Worth about half an hour earlier, a big man in buckskins on a magnificent black-and-
white Ovaro stallion. He had ridden in from the piney
woods of East Texas and was glad to get out of that humid,
mosquito-infested country.

In the cross timbers region of north central Texas, Fort
Worth had grown up around the army post of the same

name that had been founded about a dozen years earlier.
Now it was a good-sized crossroads town. Fargo had passed
through it several times in the past and knew the best
places to cut the trail dust from his throat.

As dusk settled, he left the Ovaro tied at the hitch rail
outside and entered the Top Notch Saloon on Commerce
Street intent only on getting a drink, and maybe later a
meal. If there was a good poker game going on, he might
sit in on that, too.

But he had been in the saloon only a short time when
he noticed a young man standing several feet away along
the bar, tossing back shots of whiskey. He was old enough
to drink, but he couldn't have had much experience at it.

He seemed bound and determined to make up for that,
however. He was bleary-eyed and none too steady on his
feet, and his voice was more blurred every time he ordered
another round. He wore town clothes, and his collar
seemed to be too tight. He kept tugging at it.

Fargo made it a rule not to stick his nose into other
people's business unless he was invited, and even then he
was wary about it. If that young fella wanted to drink himself into a sodden state, that was his affair.

But then Fargo's lake-blue eyes, which were noted for
their keenness all across the West, saw how three roughly
dressed men at a corner table were watching the youngster.
Their expressions were of cruel anticipation and avarice.

When the boy left the saloon, the trio of hardcases intended to follow him, jump him, and rob him. Fargo was
as sure of that as if he had overheard them talking about it.

Again, it was none of his business, but there was a chance
they might really hurt the youngster, even kill him. Fargo
was going to have a hard time doing nothing when he knew
that possibility existed.

Then the girl had come along to complicate things.

Her name was Roxanne, she told him. She had a place
upstairs where she would surely admire to take him and
show him a good time.

Fargo had been a while without a woman, and he was a
man of vast appetites for many things, including female
companionship. So he was sorely tempted.

"What do you say, honey?" she cajoled as she looked up at him with appealing green eyes. She rested a hand on his arm and rubbed it in little circles.

From this angle, Fargo had a good view down the low-cut neckline of her spangled dress. He could see most of the firm globes of lightly freckled flesh, down to the brown upper edges of her nipples.

Movement that he caught from the corner of his eye made him look around. He saw the young boozer stumbling toward an empty table, glass in hand. The fella sat down, drained the drink, and then slowly slumped forward until his head was resting on the table. A snore came from his mouth.

Fargo smiled faintly. The boy had finally shown a little sense. He wouldn't be going anywhere for a while.

"Well, what about it?" Roxanne prodded.

"Lead the way," Fargo told her.

Roxanne laughed and took hold of his hand. "I thought you were gonna make me wait all night, darlin'."

"Plenty of other men in here," Fargo commented.

She laughed again. "None of 'em that look like you, though."

Fargo wasn't vain, but he was realistic. He knew that women found his rugged good looks attractive. He didn't try to take advantage of that, but he didn't ignore it, either. With Roxanne's hand in his, he climbed a narrow set of stairs to the second floor.

A balcony overlooked the main room of the saloon, and off that balcony were small bedchambers where Roxanne and the other girls plied their trade. She opened the door to one and led Fargo inside.

The furnishings consisted of a bed—the sheets looked relatively clean, Fargo noted with approval—a chair, and a small table with a lamp and a basin on it. The lamp was already lit, the flame turned low.

After closing the door, Roxanne turned the lamp up, and its yellow glow filled the room. She turned her back to Fargo, lifted her long black hair, and said rather coyly, "Would you unbutton my dress?"

Fargo was glad to oblige. As the back of the dress came

open, he slid it down over her shoulders. Roxanne pulled her arms out of the sleeves, wiggled her hips, and pushed the dress down over her thighs. It fell to the floor around her feet.

That left her wearing only stockings and slippers. She turned to face Fargo. She hadn't been in this game long enough for it to wear on her. She was still young, fresh, and beautiful. Her breasts were high and full and firm, crowned by dark brown nipples. The thatch of hair between her legs was as dark as that on her head.

She came into Fargo's arms and tilted her head up for his kiss. Her lips parted eagerly under the probing caress of his tongue. He rested one hand on the smooth skin between her shoulder blades while the other slid down her back to the curve of her hips.

She surged against him, molding her body to his through the buckskins he wore. His shaft quickly grew hard, and she slipped a hand between them to caress it. A low moan came from deep in her throat as she explored him and realized how much of him was waiting for her.

She drew her head back and gasped, "Oh, my God, Skye! I can't wait!"

He bent slightly, slipped an arm around the backs of her thighs, and straightened, picking her up and slinging her face down over his shoulder. That put her lovely rump right next to his ear. He gave it a little slap as he turned around and walked over to the bed.

Then, with one swift, unexpected movement, he dumped her on the mattress and said, "I'm afraid you're going to have to wait a while, Roxanne."

Then he turned to the door.

"What . . . what are you doing?" she exclaimed as she sprawled nude, lovely, and confused on the bed. "Where are you going?"

"There's something I have to do," Fargo told her over his shoulder. "Stay right there."

He didn't know if she would do as he told her or not, but right now, he didn't care. He stepped out onto the balcony and his eyes swept the crowded room below him.

Just as he expected, the young man who had been drinking so heavily was no longer dozing at the table. Nor was he to be seen anywhere else in the saloon.

As Fargo stood there, his hands clenched on the balcony railing, a shot blasted somewhere in the night outside the saloon. The hubbub inside the Top Notch muffled the sound, but Fargo heard and recognized it.

His long legs took him to the stairs and then down, two at a time. When he reached the bottom he started across the room, shouldering men out of the way, ignoring their angry, startled reactions. He made it to the door and slapped the batwings aside. Pausing as he stepped onto the boardwalk, he listened intently.

The sounds of a struggle, accompanied by harsh voices raised in anger, came from a dark patch of shadows to his right. As he came to the black mouth of an alley, he heard a man bark, "Watch it! Grab him, damn it! He's getting away!"

Running footsteps pounded toward Fargo. As his eyes adjusted to the darkness, he saw a figure loom up from the shadows and stagger toward him. But then the man's feet got tangled up with each other and he pitched forward, slamming hard to the ground.

The impact must have stunned the fleeing man, because he didn't move. Three more shapes appeared behind him, closing in on him.

"Now we've got him," one of the men growled.

Fargo took a step toward them and said, "No, what you've got is trouble."

The three men stiffened. Fargo had no doubt that they were the hardcases he had seen in the saloon, just as he was certain the man lying senseless on the ground was the youngster who had been pouring Who-hit-John down his gullet.

"Back off, mister," came the low-voice warning. "This is none of your business."

"You're right," Fargo said. "I reckon that makes me a damn fool, but so be it. Back off and leave the boy alone."

The man standing farthest back suddenly said, "Kill 'em both!"

Colt flame bloomed in the darkness of the alley. Fargo

went to a knee behind a rain barrel. A slug chewed off splinters that stung Fargo's face. The Colt roared and bucked in his hand as he thumbed off several swift shots.

One man yelled in pain; another let out a low groan. Fargo heard a bullet whistle past his head as another slug thumped into the caked mud beside him.

The young man started to stir. His senses were coming back after being knocked out of him by his hard fall. He was lying in the open, too vulnerable to all the lead flying around.

Fargo carried out the border shift, tossing his gun from right hand to left, catching it in midair and firing less than a heartbeat later. At the same time he reached out and grabbed the young man's collar with his right hand.

The muscles of Fargo's arm and shoulders bunched under the buckskin shirt as he hauled the youngster out of the middle of the alley and into the meager protection of the rain barrel. A bullet clipped Fargo's hat while he was doing that and sent it spinning off his head.

With a grunt of effort, Fargo half-threw and half-rolled the young man against the wall of the building. He had only one shot left in the Colt's cylinder, and it didn't look like there would be time to reload. The man who had been giving the orders barked another command.

"Rush 'em!"

The other men hesitated. Fargo knew he had wounded at least one of them, and clearly they didn't relish the prospect of charging straight toward his gun. He was ready to use that last bullet and then pull the Arkansas Toothpick from the sheath strapped to his calf. He could do a lot of damage with the knife's long, heavy, razor-sharp blade.

It wasn't going to come to that, though, because curious shouts sounded from the mouth of the alley. Townspeople were coming to see what all the shooting was about, and the would-be killers didn't want that many witnesses around.

Fargo heard a muttered curse, and then the leader of the hardcases snapped, "Let's get out of here!"

The command was followed by the thud of rapid footsteps retreating along the hard-packed dirt of the alley.

Fargo could have sent a shot after them to hurry them

along, but he didn't bother. They were already fleeing. He was unhurt, and he hoped the young man he had rescued wasn't seriously injured, either.

"Get a lantern!" a man yelled out on Commerce Street. "Somebody's been murdered back there in the alley!"

Well, that wasn't exactly the case, thought Fargo. The young man moaned and tried to sit up. Fargo quickly reloaded the Colt, then holstered it and took the youngster's arm.

"Are you hit?" he asked as he helped the young man sit up.

"I . . . I don't think so. But I . . . oh, Lord! . . . I'm gonna be sick—"

Fargo stood and stepped back as the young man retched against the wall. The alley didn't smell too good to start with, and the stink got worse.

Flickering light washed over the huddled figure as several men came down the alley, one of them carrying a lantern. Fargo saw that the other men carried shotguns and rifles. They were ready for whatever trouble they might find.

"Take it easy, boys," Fargo told them in a low, powerful voice. "The ruckus is over."

"What happened?" one of the men asked. He was fat, with a walrus mustache hanging down over his mouth. In the lantern light, Fargo saw that he had a star pinned to his vest.

"Three men jumped this fella here," Fargo explained, nodding toward the young man as he spoke. The youngster had stopped throwing up and was trying to push himself to his feet by leaning against the wall of the building. He was still unsteady, but not as drunk as he had been.

"There was a lot of shootin'," the local lawman said. "Either of you need a sawbones?"

Fargo shook his had. "I don't. I'm pretty sure he wasn't hit, either."

The youngster had made it to his feet. He leaned against the wall and shook his head. His face was covered with sweat, and he was pale as milk.

"I'm all right," he managed to say. "Just . . . just feel a mite poorly."

Excerpt from *TEXAS TERROR TRAIL*

The lawman snorted. "Hell, you look like death warmed over, son. What you need is a pot o' good strong black coffee."

The young man moaned and hunched over, but there was nothing left in his stomach to come up.

"Don't I know you?" the lawman went on. "You're the Forrestal boy, aren't you?"

The youngster nodded shakily. "Yeah. Vance Forrestal."

Fargo had never heard of him before, but evidently the name was known in Fort Worth.

The lawman swung toward Fargo. "Who are you, mister, and what's your part in this?"

Fargo answered the second question first. "I saw this young fella in the Top Notch Saloon tossing back the whiskey, and I had a hunch he might wind up in trouble. My name's Skye Fargo."

"Huh," the badge-toter said. "I know that name. You're the one they call the Trailsman."

Fargo nodded. "That they do, sometimes."

"How'd you know somebody was after young Forrestal here?"

"I saw some men in the saloon watching him. They looked like hardcases, and I could tell by the way they acted they were thinking about robbing him."

"Wasn't . . . wasn't what they were after," Forrestal said fuzzily. "They wanted me *dead*."

That was the way it had seemed to Fargo, too, during the heat of battle in the alley. He knew his first impression in the saloon had been wrong. And he was curious why the three men had wanted to kill Vance Forrestal.

But he was curious about a few other things, too, and he wanted answers to those questions before he made up his mind about what was going on here.

"If you don't need me anymore, Sheriff . . ."

"Hold on there," the lawman said sharply as Fargo started toward the mouth of the alley. "I ain't done with you, Fargo. And I'm the town marshal, not the sheriff. Bert Hinchcliffe's the name."

"Sorry, Marshal," Fargo said. "I always try to cooperate with the law."

But the delay was chafing at him, and he wanted to get

174

back to the saloon. He had a hunch at least some of the answers he wanted were waiting for him there.

"You said you saw three hardcases in the saloon," Hinchcliffe went on. "Are you sure it was the same fellas you swapped lead with out here in the alley?"

"I'm convinced it was, but I couldn't answer to it in court," Fargo said. "It was too dark to get a good look at them."

"What did they look like? The ones in the Top Notch, I mean."

Quickly, Fargo described the three men as best he could, although there hadn't been that much to distinguish them. They were just the sort of hard-faced, beard-stubbled, roughly dressed men who could be found drifting across the West almost anywhere.

Marshal Hinchcliffe turned to Vance Forrestal. "What about you? Did you recognize anybody while you was drinkin'?"

Forrestal shook his head and grimaced at the pain the movement caused him. "No, but you've got to remember, Marshal, I was pretty drunk."

"You ain't quite sober yet, I'd wager," Hinchcliffe said dryly.

The young man hiccuped. "N-no, Marshal, I'm not. But I'm getting there."

"How come you said those hombres wanted to kill you, instead of just robbin' you?"

Forrestal frowned. "Did I say that? I must have been mistaken. I'm sure they were just . . . just ordinary robbers and c-cutthroats."

Now that was a mite interesting, thought Fargo. Vance Forrestal was changing his story. A few minutes ago, the three hardcases had been assassins. Now they were merely thieves.

Why had Forrestal taken back his accusation?

Fargo didn't know, but again, he thought he might find the answer, or at least a clue, in the saloon. He said impatiently, "Look Marshal, there's nothing else I can tell you."

"Yeah, all right." Hinchcliffe waved a hand. "You can go, Fargo. You plan to be around Fort Worth for a while?"

"At least tonight. After that I don't know," Fargo answered honestly.

"Reckon I can't hold you to any more than that."

Before leaving the alley, Fargo put a hand on Vance Forrestal's shoulder and asked, "You sure you're all right?"

The young man nodded. "Yeah. Thanks, Mister . . . Fargo, was it?"

"*De nada.* Better watch that boozing in the future."

"Yeah." Forrestal nodded glumly. "You're sure right about that."

Fargo walked out of the alley before the marshal could think of some reason to stop him. He went quickly back to the saloon. Several of the patrons asked him what had happened outside, but he ignored them as he went over to the bar.

The man standing behind the hardwood regarded him nervously. "Something I can do you for, mister?" the bartender asked.

"Roxanne still upstairs?" Fargo asked. He had already looked around the room and confirmed that the dark-haired beauty was nowhere in sight.

The bartender shrugged. "I don't know. I don't keep up with those soiled doves, mister."

Fargo started to nod, but then his hand shot out and bunched in the bartender's dirty apron. He jerked the man forward, pulling him halfway onto the bar. The bartender yelled a curse and flailed, trying to reach under the bar.

Fargo figured the man was trying to get his hands on a bungstarter or some other weapon. Stooping slightly, the Trailsman grasped the wooden grips of the Arkansas Toothpick and slid the big knife out of its sheath. He pressed the tip of the blade against the bartender's throat, just hard enough to make his point without breaking the skin.

"Now," Fargo said, "I'll ask you again. Is Roxanne still upstairs?"

"I . . . I don't know! Be careful with that knife, mister! Ohhhh . . ."

"Let me worry about the knife," Fargo advised. "You just worry about telling me the truth."

The saloon had gone quiet as Fargo held the knife to the bartender's throat. From the corner of his eye Fargo saw a couple of men edging around, trying to get behind him. Probably bouncers, he thought.

"Better tell your boys to stay back," Fargo warned the bartender. "If anybody was to jump me, I might just shove this Toothpick clean through your neck before I knew what was going on."

He wasn't going to do that, of course. But the bartender didn't know it was a bluff. He choked out, "Stay back! Do what he says!"

"Last time," Fargo intoned ominously. "Roxanne?"

"I don't know!" the bartender asked. "I told her to get out of here when she came down after you left! She went back upstairs, and that's the last I seen of her!"

"You were the one who sicced her on me in the first place, right?"

"I . . . I told her to see if she could get you upstairs!"

"Because you noticed me watching that young fella and the three men who were keeping an eye on him. You were in on it with them, weren't you?"

That accusation was partially guesswork on Fargo's part, but he was confident that he was right.

"I . . . I don't know anything about what happened outside! I just knew they didn't want anybody interfering with them."

"They paid you off to see that Forrestal left here drunk as a skunk?"

The bartender tried to shake his head but flinched away from the point of the blade as he did so Fargo pressed it home inexorably.

"They didn't have to pay me for that! The kid's a boozer, everybody knows that! But they slipped me a few bucks to see that nobody mixed in. I . . . I saw the way you were watchin' them, and I recognized you as Skye Fargo. I know your reputation, mister."

"Where do you know me from?" Fargo asked.

"I saw you a couple of years ago . . . up in Missouri . . . you killed three men in a stand-up gunfight . . . Please, Fargo, don't kill me!"

Fargo leaned closer to him. "One more question. Forrestal was sleeping it off when I went upstairs. Why did he wake up and leave?"

"They . . . they took him out of here! Acted like they were his friends, they did. Said they'd go dunk him in the horse trough and sober him up."

"You knew damn well that wasn't what they had in mind," Fargo grated. "You let them take him out of here to his death."

"Th-the kid's dead?"

"No, but it's no thanks to you that he's not." Fargo gave the man a hard shove that sent him sliding off the bar and stumbling back into a row of shelves lined with liquor bottles. Several tipped over from the impact and shattered on the floor.

"I swear, Fargo, I didn't know what they were going to do! I don't want any trouble in here."

"Too late for that," Fargo growled.

He swung away from the bar and sheathed the Arkansas Toothpick. The crowd parted as he made his way toward the stairs. He didn't expect to find Roxanne, but he was going to check the room where she had taken him.

He was only halfway there when he heard yells and scrambling behind him. Twisting around, he saw that the bartender had pulled a sawed-off shotgun from under the bar.

"Pull a knife on me, will you, you bastard!" he shouted as he jerked the barrels of the deadly weapon toward Fargo.

No other series has this much historical action!

THE TRAILSMAN

Available wherever books are sold or at
www.penguin.com

GRITTY HISTORICAL ACTION FROM
USA TODAY BESTSELLING AUTHOR

RALPH
COTTON